For friends and loved ones

KILL
THE
BABYSITTER

CHAPTER 1

March 2019

Jane Freeman was washing paint brushes in the sink when the Beast attacked her in broad daylight. Six feet of puffy, ruddy skin and brown eyes that simmered with hatred, the Beast wanted her dead from day one.

Everyone has had that one bully that scared the living daylights of them, that forced you to fake a sick day or beg your parents to homeschool you. But by the time you reach adulthood, the memories of those horrid people mostly fade away — or send you to therapy or the bottle. In the moment, all you can do is try to survive.

The Beast stalked the halls of Morganville High looking for trouble. Looking for Jane. Tall, wide, and menacing, the Beast was built like a rugby player. In just the few months she had been attending Jane's school, the

Beast had made Jane's life a living hell. Jane had no idea what she had done to incur the much bigger, stronger girl's wrath, but sometimes it didn't matter who you were. Anyone could get caught in the grinding wheel of high school.

That wheel had ground Jane down enough for several lifetimes. Her parents had divorced, and she hadn't seen her dad in years; her mom worked long, late nights at the hospital in town. She was a C-student with a paper due every damn week. And she was seventeen without a car, forced to take the bus to school and her feet everywhere else.

All she could do was fantasize about her dream car, a hot blue Mustang with black leather seats. Then she would be free, driving across the U.S. to retrace the old Route 66. And then she could finally have some fun.

Until then, she had to endure the Beast, and up until that Tuesday afternoon, she had been doing very well at avoiding her. They only shared two classes a week: Miss Smithers' chill-as-fuck art hour.

Maybe things had been going too well in the class. Jane was getting Bs (Miss Smithers handed 'em out like candy if her students simply applied themselves) and arguing less with the popular kids about the music they played. (Emily Burke and Brad Polanski and their goons swarmed the big table by the stereo so they could control the music, and they played Drake's droning, monotonous bullshit every chance they got, and then they shat over Jane's suggestions to play Ozzy and Led Zeppelin.)

So that Tuesday morning, when it was Jane's turn to wash the brushes at the end of class, she mindlessly hummed one of the less annoying Drake songs. A heavy set of hands slammed against her back — the Beast's paws! Turning to see, Jane knocked her hip against the counter.

"Ow!" she yelped

The Beast's puffy, red face was too close. Her hot, post-lunch breath blew into Jane's face. *"Leave me alone,"* she growled, before shoving Jane again.

Jane fell against the sink. The other students screeched back in their chairs, ooh-ing excitedly as they gathered around. The phones they weren't supposed to have in class came out in droves, clutched in trembling hands as a hush fell over the room. Everyone understood this wasn't the time for wisecracks.

It was time for a fight.

Jane gripped the brushes, watching the Beast stomp away. Her hip throbbed and her back itched where the Beast slammed into her. Her ego raged red-hot.

Without a second to think, she threw the brushes at the Beast's back. The Beast spun around, teeth gritted.

Jane turned to flee. Her sneakered foot landed on one of the brushes, and she skidded, falling face first onto the popular kids' table. Emily leaned in with her camera as Jane almost crashed into her.

"Extreme close-up," cracked a cute brown-haired boy. Nate-something. His blue eyes shined as he flashed her a grin. He only registered in Jane's world because her friend

Lily wouldn't stop gushing about him.

"What is going on in here?!" cried Miss Smithers as Jane picked herself up.

The Beast fled the room.

After the conflict simmered down, the principal and Miss Smithers sent Jane to the nurse's office. She laid on a cot in the dimly lit nurse's office, holding a bag of ice against her hip, jeans pulled down low. The nurse asked her a million questions that her mom would probably ask when she got home. Eventually the nurse had to slip out to deal with another student and Jane got to lay back and stare at the ceiling.

She wondered what they were doing to the Beast. The girl was probably being yelled at by Principal Hector. Then she would be suspended, maybe even expelled. The school had a "no tolerance" policy for bullying and fighting — but that was only if the *school* determined it was bullying.

Regardless, Jane couldn't help but smile, imagining being free of that horrible girl for the rest of the year.

After about an hour of lounging around, Jane had company. The nurse shuffled in with the cute boy from art class. Nate. He sat down on the opposite cot and smiled shyly, trying not to notice that Jane's jeans were pulled down, exposing her bony, bruised hip. She didn't feel very voluptuous, but the blush that crept up his face made her feel self-conscious.

As soon as the nurse was gone, she sat up and adjusted her clothes. "Hey," she said.

"Hey," he said right back.

"What're you in for?"

He grinned and rolled up his pant leg. "Sprained ankle."

It didn't look swollen or hurt in any way. It looked like a teenage boy's hairy, skinny ankle. "Uh, what?"

The nurse poked her head back into the room. Age had etched deep, angry lines into her dour face. "No talking."

Both students nodded and waited until she was gone. Then Nate took a seat on her rolling stool and cruised closer to Jane. Keeping his voice low, he said, "I just wanted to see the girl who slayed the Beast."

Slayed? Jane had replayed the fight over and over as she sat in purgatory. All she had done was throw brushes at the girl. She didn't commit murder. "What're you talking about?"

"The Beast is gone," he said. "The principal keeps calling her to the office. Haven't you heard?"

Jane had not. The nurse's office was the only room in the building that didn't have a speaker for the PA system. All she heard was muffled announcements from the hallway.

But she didn't believe the Beast was gone. More like "escaped." The Beast was loose.

She swallowed, thoughts flying through her mind at a mile a minute. "I need a car," she muttered.

She had needed a car since the Beast first started intimidating her. Following her home from school on a few occasions. When she tried taking the bus, the Beast would be there too. But a car was the ultimate safe space. The Beast couldn't get her then.

"I could give you a ride…"

She looked up. A ride was currency, but it was also used to barter. Cash, grass, or ass — nobody rides for free. She gave him a side-eyed look, summoning her usual bravado. "Sorry. I don't take rides from strangers."

"Even if I have candy?" he said with that damned grin.

Jane couldn't help it. She grinned back, running a hand through her messy, black curls. *No wonder Lily likes this guy. He's kinda cute.* "What's your name?" she asked, as if she didn't know.

"Nate Crawford," he said. Then he did something weird — he reached out to shake her hand. She let him, but no one had ever done that before. His skin was warm and dry, and he held her just long enough to make her blush. When he let go, she almost floated off the cot. "I'm pretty new here. Just moved last month. And you're Jane Freeman."

"Yeah. How'd you know that?"

He shrugged. "I've seen you around."

"Oh," was all she could say. "Cool."

"About that ride? I can't take you very far. Also promised a friend I'd drive him to yoga. But if you don't trust me — *yet* — bring a friend. I'll get you outta here safe and sound. It could be fun."

Stroking her chin, she pretended to mull it over. "Yeah, okay. I could use some fun."

CHAPTER 2

Lily followed on Jane's heels after the final bell. Jane's mother didn't raise a dummy; if Jane was going to hitch a ride with a boy she barely knew, then she would definitely drag a friend with her. But Jane was beginning to think that if she could survive the Beast, maybe she could survive anything.

She wasn't home free yet. The Beast weighed heavily on her mind as the two girls sneaked out of the school and cut across the parking lot toward Nate's gray Volkswagen Golf. As soon as Jane spotted him, she stood a little straighter and gave him a wave. There was no reason for Nate to think she was chickenshit.

"Over here!" he hollered, waving back.

Hunched over her backpack, which she clung to like a life preserver, Lily tugged on Jane's elbow. The parking lot was full of cars even as students poured out of the building. They should be safe in the crowd, but Jane stayed on high alert.

"I can't believe you talked to *Nate,*" Lily said in a hushed but excited voice. "I tried saying hello last week, but Emily's friends have their hooks in him."

Someone tall darted between them. Jane flinched. For a heart-stopping moment, she was certain the Beast had caught up to her. But it was only Troy Manders, his yoga mat rolled up and hanging off his shoulder. He gave Nate a high five before taking the front seat.

"Oh, great," Jane muttered. "Troy's coming too."

"You said he had to drive a friend..." Lily reminded her.

"Yeah, but I didn't think it was that asshole." She put on a big smile as they approached Nate's car. "Hey."

Nate grinned. "Hey," he replied, as he opened the back door for them. "I didn't think you were gonna make it."

"What do you mean? Of course—" Jane paused to see what Nate was nodding at.

Behind them, not far off from the route they had taken through the lot, was a tall oak tree. All spindly branches, the tree was bereft of leaves and life. On warmer days, it was a hangout for stoners or Emily's crew, or a mix of both. On this bitterly cold March day, the Beast lurked under its faint shadow.

"Shit." *Now what?*

"Come on," said Nate, ushering them inside.

Troy rolled his window down, smacking the side of the car. "Come on. I don't got all day."

Nostrils flaring, the Beast rose up on her haunches. Her big hands squeezed the straps of her Jansport backpack. The distance between the two enemies was suddenly too short. Jane pushed Lily into the backseat and tumbled in after her. Nate got in the driver's seat and revved the engine. He peeled out, locking the doors as they sped past the Beast.

"Close one," said Nate, checking his mirrors.

"Holy shit," breathed Jane, twisting around to look back. The Beast stare after them. The wind blew her sandy red hair around her wide face.

Once they were far enough away from the school that they couldn't see the building, Nate pulled over. "Sorry I can't take you home," he said. "I promised Troy—"

"Yeah, yeah," Troy said, cutting him off. "They know."

"It's cool," said Jane, climbing out and sliding her backpack onto her shoulders. "You didn't even have to do this much."

Lily nodded in agreement.

"See you tomorrow?" he asked.

Jane shrugged, trying to feign a coolness she didn't possess. "Maybe." And then she walked away. Nate's car remained still for a beat as Jane strode away with Lily fumbling after her. She didn't even glance back when he drove off, waving as he passed.

"Oh my gawd!" Lily covered her gaping mouth. "I can't believe we were in Nate Crawford's car! I'm freaking out!"

Jane shrugged again, even though her stomach tingled at the thought of seeing him again. "He's just another guy. No big deal."

"To *you,* maybe. But he's so cute!"

"Yeah, but he hangs out with Troy."

"So?"

"Troy is the biggest caveman loser."

"He's not so bad…"

Jane scoffed. "You're only saying that because you wanna hang out with Nate so bad."

"I think being around Nate is making Troy a better person. He's so much more well-rounded now. Did you know that he started taking drama and guitar this term?"

"And yoga and art. So what? You put a paintbrush in his hand, he's still a neanderthal."

"Yeah, and you're the one who called him a dudebro last year. I guess he's trying hard not to be one."

Jane kicked a clump of muddy snow out of her path. "What does he care what I think?"

"Everyone cares what someone thinks."

Jane wondered what all the popular people thought of her. She tried not to seem eager to join their snotty ranks, but at the same time, she was curious what her life would be like. Maybe it would be easier because she would have more people to defend her against mean bitch monsters.

About to ask that question, she glanced over at Lily. But Lily was already chewing on her lip and staring at the ground. Her long, pale hair hung down the front of her puffy coat, tangled and frayed from the wind. The trouble with Lily was that she couldn't be anything less than honest, but she also wouldn't dare say anything mean about anyone, especially her best friend. That meant she was caught in a catch-22 whenever Jane asked her opinion. Her only way out was to say nothing at all and wait for the earth to open up and swallow her whole.

So Jane gave her an out and asked if she wanted to get something to eat.

"I can't tonight," she said. "I'm babysitting."

"I battled the Beast today and you're going to wipe a bunch of snotty noses?"

She looked down at her backpack. "No... Not a bunch, just two. They're pretty nice kids. They always go to bed early and leave me alone. And their parents pay pretty well too."

Had Jane been a cartoon, dollar signs would have sprung up in her eyes. "How much?"

Lily bit her lip. "Um, $20 an hour."

"Holy shit! Wait — for how many hours?"

"Uh, three or four?"

"Holy shit!" Jane made a running start toward the Patriquin's big apple tree. She pretended to attempt a running backflip but stumbled at the last moment only to land on her feet. Like always. "Holy shit! That's eighty bucks!"

Lily nodded, clutching her book bag straps. "And sometimes there's snacks."

"I don't care about snacks," said Jane, waving the words away. "I need money."

Money meant she could buy a car. She wouldn't have to run out of school as soon as the bell rang just to avoid the Beast. She wouldn't be caught dead on the street if she ran into the girl at the convenience store. She would be free. Untouchable.

"So you're going to become a babysitter?" asked Lily.

Jane shrugged. "Hell, yeah. Why not? Sounds easy enough."

"You really think so? It's actually pretty hard when the kids won't listen to you. And you have to take the babysitter's course."

"A course? What for?"

"You have to know about safety and stuff in case there's an emergency."

"Okay, what do I do?"

"You sign up at the community hall. They usually do one once a month, on a Saturday, I think? And it's only eight hours."

Jane's face fell. *"On a Saturday?* Jeez."

Mr. Patriquin peeked through his curtains at the two teens lingering on the sidewalk outside his house. Lily started walking, hoping Jane would follow so the old man wouldn't yell at them. But Jane held her ground.

"Fine, so okay," she said. "I guess I'll have to do the course."

"It's $60."

"What the fuck?" Jane groaned so loudly that Mr. Patriquin banged on his window. Loitering teens were one thing, but *swearing* teens who loitered were bad news. She wouldn't be surprised if he called the cops. So she followed Lily, turning at the end of his property line to shoot him a sassy smirk.

Then she shook her head, returning to her conversation with Lily. "Damn. Sixty bucks? That's like all the profit from your first gig! That's not fair."

"My mom says to think of it as an investment."

"Investment? Into what — a lame job you're only going to have until college?"

Lily swept her hair behind her ears and stared at the ground. "Well, I like it," she squeaked.

Jane didn't hear her because she was busy running numbers in her head. She struggled with math, but when it came to calculating her own imaginary income, she could math with the best of them.

"What if I don't do the course?" she asked.

Lily's eyes bulged. "But you have to."

"How would anybody know?"

"They'll ask."

"So? They don't need to know the truth. It's not like it's illegal."

Lily stopped dead in her tracks. "You can't. That's wrong. And what if there's an emergency? You won't know what to do!"

"What kind of emergency? Like I run out of Pepsi? Boo hoo."

"I mean a *real one*. Like a fire or someone gets hurt?"

Jane crossed her arms, sticking out a hip. "And how many times have you had to put out a fire or deal with an injured kid?"

"It's not that simple…"

She shrugged. "You just call 911. No big deal, right?"

Lily went back to chewing on her lip. The bottom part was a dried, peeling mess after talking to Jane about babysitting. She couldn't say what bothered her because that meant telling Jane that she would make an awful babysitter, and Lily just didn't have the guts to say it.

"Now how do I get one of these gigs?" Jane asked.

CHAPTER 3

Jane and Lily visited the supermarket community board. In the stuffy vestibule, they gazed up at the large cork bulletin board littered with printouts of missing pets and buy-and-sell ads. In between the chaos were postings for babysitters.

Overwhelmed by the amount of information, Jane grew distracted by a FOR SALE sign. She ripped it free from its thumbtack and waved it in Lily's face. "Oh, shit! It's a Mustang. *A blue* Mustang!" The owner was asking for $3,900 for a 1999 model.

Lily skimmed the information. "It's manual. You don't know manual."

"I'll learn," she replied. "It's my dream car! I'd be stupid to pass up this offer." The possibility of owning her very own Mustang in less than fifty hours of sitting only hardened her resolve. "I gotta find some kids."

"How about this one?" Lily pointed to an ad. *Babysitter wanted. Two kids. Must have own vehicle.* "Oops, sorry."

"They want me to have my own car *to start?* That's bullshit. I'm not driving no booger bandits around in my Mustang. Fuck that." She tapped her finger on another detail in that ad. "Also — minimum wage."

"Well, that's kinda the norm," said Lily. "You don't have much experience…"

"Here we go!" Jane ripped another paper from the board. "'$25 an hour.'"

The gig was in Sunshine Falls, Morganville's richy-rich neighbourhood. The parent, Bree Harker, needed a sitter to watch her three kids. Mainly weekends, occasionally weeknights. There were other details attached (including the requirement for completion of a babysitting course), but Jane could only see the dollar signs — and one more obstacle.

Reference required.

Jane grinned. "What if…"

Lily blinked. "What?"

"What if you be my reference?"

"And say what? You've never watched a kid in your whole life."

"Come on, Lil — do this for me, please?" She laced her fingers together, begging. She would have gotten down on her knees, but mud and melted snow turned the flour into a slippery mess, and she didn't want to ruin her jeans. "Please?"

"I-I don't want to lie…"

"You don't have to! Just tell them the facts. Say that while I'm new, I *am* enthusiastic. And good with kids."

"But you're not—"

"We don't know that for sure," said Jane, "but I might have it within me. Like a Mary Poppins instinct, or something."

"I don't know…"

Jane grinned. Lily's uncertainty was as good as yes. Her resolve was a mountain of mud, ready to slide down and give way to everything. All Jane had to do was keep pouring it on.

Lily sighed.

Jane called the number and spoke to Mrs. Harker, giving Lily as a reference before the woman ended the call. Within seconds, Lily's phone rang. She gasped, fumbling to answer it. Mrs. Harker was quick to check references.

Trembling, she held out the phone. "What do I say?"

"Just answer it," Jane sighed.

Lily stammered and paused while her thumb clumsily jabbed at the screen too many times. Jane finally took it from her and answered, holding it to Lily's head. "Uh, yeah?" said Lily, whose face turned cherry red. "It's me. I mean, hello?"

Jane leaned in, listening as Mrs. Harker explained why she was calling.

"Y-yes, I know Jane. She's really good… Uh-huh… Uh-huh… She's new, but she's, um, enthusiastic? And good with kids...?" She bit her ragged lip. "Um, sure."

Nervous Lily prattled on while Jane began spending the money she hadn't yet earned. It occurred to her that she was going to have to do an honest three or four hours of work to make bank, and that meant figuring out how to babysit. She didn't even ask how old the kids were. What if they were tiny babies? Jane had never even held a baby before. What if she had to change diapers too?

She was starting to get cold feet about this whole thing. Maybe trying to get a burger-flipping job at A&W wouldn't be so bad. The burgers never cried at you or shit themselves.

Before she could tell Lily to hang up and forget it, Lily ended the call. Her face crumpled and she covered her eyes. "Oh, my god. I can't believe I just did that! That was the worst!"

Jane's phone rang. She stared at the screen. *B. HARKER*. All she had to do was ignore it.

Lily peeked out. "Well? Are you gonna answer it?"

"Well..."

"You better answer it! You made me say those things! It was embarrassing! I lied for you!"

"Alright, alright." She answered it. "Hello? Oh, hi, Mrs. Harker. Thanks for— Oh, hey, Saturday? Well, actually, I've got—"

Jane had plans to coerce Lily into taking her to see a movie in Edgarton, but the other girl glared at her, willing her to take the job Jane desperately wanted minutes ago.

"Yeah, I'm free. I'll be there."

* * *

Come Saturday night, Jane's stomach twisted and turned. It wasn't that she was getting sick or that she ate something bad; she was nervous. Ever since taking on the babysitting gig, she began questioning herself and her abilities. She could bullshit her way through any list of problems, but doubted childminding was on it.

She lounged in bed most of the day until her mom announced that she was leaving for work. Jane rolled out of bed and dragged herself down to the kitchen, where she poured herself a bowl of Froot Loops.

Tanis Freeman breezed through, planting a quick kiss on Jane's mop of dark, curly hair. "So proud of you, honey."

"Why?" she asked, shovelling a spoon of rainbow loops into her mouth.

"It's your first real job."

"Selling Girl Guide cookies didn't count?"

Tanis, dressed in scrubs for her double shift at the hospital, frowned. "Janie — selling cookies is part of being a Guide. It's not actually a job."

"I remember the shitty uniform," she muttered.

"Hey! Watch it."

"I said *itchy*," she lied.

Tanis gave her daughter a knowing glare, forcing Jane to keep her head down. When Tanis was halfway out the door, she turned back and warned, "Watch your language around those kids tonight. I don't want you to lose your job because of your rampant potty mouth."

Jane smiled mischievously. "I'll be good."

"And how are you getting there?"

Because the blue Mustang was many babysitting gigs away from being within her grasp, Jane had to figure out another way to get to the Harkers' house in Sunshine Falls. Jane had never been, but she heard it was pretty nice.

And because the neighbourhood was so nice, that meant it was far away from their lousy condo townhouse. So Jane was stuck walking, which meant she should have left five minutes ago.

"Don't worry, Mom," she said, as her mom ran out the door to make it to her own shift on time. "I got it figured out."

She dumped her bowl of half-eaten cereal into the sink, grabbed her coat, and marched into the backyard. Near the back of the yard, a rusted tin-roof shed slumped against a tree.

When Tanis bought the little townhouse unit a few years ago, they were coming from nothing. Jane's had dad left, and they had been stuck living with her aunt while her mom finished nursing school. It took a couple of years of scrimping and saving, but after that, Tanis had finally saved up enough for a down payment on a modest piece-of-crap townhouse on the west side.

Surrounded by newer single-family homes, the townhouse complex had been built in a late '70s housing boom. It was an ugly, brown eyesore of 171-units jammed with working-class families forced to commute into the city as they busted their asses to own something.

Their unit's previous owner left behind the shed. It should have been condemned. The roof leaked and squirrels hoarded pinecones if you didn't properly close the door. One year, Tanis encouraged Jane to clean it out and sell anything she could find. She proposed it as a great way for Jane to make some extra money, instead of hounding her for an allowance all summer long.

At the time, Jane had a painful crush on her older neighbour. Danny was in eleventh grade at the time and wore muscle shirts when the weather got warm. She would have dropped dead if he cruised by in his Jeep and saw her hosting the saddest yard sale ever.

So instead, she threw out everything she could carry and tidied up the rest, shutting it all away so neither she nor her mom had to look at it.

But in the act of cleaning, she found an old bike. She pedalled it around the complex for a bit and even walked it down to the gas station to fill up the tires. Riding it back home, she thought about using it to get to school — and then Danny sped by and chuckled.

The first time he had ever paid her any mind and he fucking laughed at her.

The bike remained in the shed for three years — until today. Without any other transportation options, Jane trampled through the snow mold and soggy dead grass to yank open the rusty sliding door and drag out the bike. She wiped off the damp, cracked seat with her elbow and climbed on. The bike squeaked, wobbling under her unsteady legs. The ride to the gas station had felt different when the concrete had been dry, when the streets had not hid potholes under dense clumps of snow and ice.

She paused to plug her ear pods in and cue up a new playlist, "MoneyMaker$" — the first track was Pink Floyd's "Money." Instead of giving in to her nerves, she took a deep breath and focused on all the money she was going to make, and all the snacks and sodas she was going to stuff into her face after she put the kids to bed, and all the bad TV she was going to binge while she waited for Mrs. Harker to come home.

Babysitting was going to be a piece of cake. Maybe even fun.

Maybe not, she thought. *But at least I've got Lily.* Lily would know what to do, and thankfully, she was usually always on her phone.

Pedalling faster and faster, Jane smiled. But her nervous stomach remained.

CHAPTER 4

The three Harker children peered down at Jane from behind the white balusters at the top of the staircase. Their sharp eyes volleyed between Jane and their mother, whose posture was impeccably straight.

Bree Harker's dark hair was pulled back in a slick, tight bun, stretching her face back. She wore a simple black dress that cost more than anything Jane would ever own. She looked stunning, but tired and stressed. The fine lines on her face told the story of a self-sufficient boss bitch who was raising three kids on her own.

She delivered her instructions to Jane as she would to one of her company's interns, with no nonsense and little room for questions. She gave a complete rundown of the house and the children. Never "my children" or "my kids" — *the children.*

Jane nodded, struggling to retain all the information

while distracted by the three sets of eyes spying on her. One of them snickered, diverting her attention from Mrs. Harker, who snapped her fingers.

"Are you listening to me?"

Jane blinked, mouth agape. "Uh, yeah." *Don't snap at me, lady. I'm not a dog.*

"Good, because I don't have many rules, but I require you to listen so you understand. These rules are important. They keep my children safe and ensure their good behaviour doesn't waver."

"Yes, ma'am."

She beckoned Jane to follow her into the kitchen. Jane, feeling even more like a dog, followed. At least she was going to get a tour of snack paradise. She stuffed her hands into her pockets to keep from rubbing them together expectantly.

Mrs. Harker opened the fridge, removing a single bottle of water. The fancy Fiji kind that Jane heard tasted like heaven. *Probably just tap water*, she thought.

Mrs. Harker excused herself to take a delicate sip.

Jane's shoulders slumped when she peeked inside the fridge. *No snacks.* Just two shelves of expensive water and fresh vegetables crammed into every free space. Not a can of pop anywhere. No cake leftovers or pizza boxes. It was so clean and green.

Her stomach rumbled. *I'm gonna starve. I don't even have money to order a pizza. Maybe she'll pay me up front.* But getting paid up front only to spend half of it on pizza was seriously going to cut into her profits.

"The children have already had dinner," said Mrs. Harker, "if you're wondering about feeding them."

I was so not thinking that. "Yeah, good." She noted a small door next to the fridge was ajar. "And if they need a snack?"

Mrs. Harker frowned and shut the pantry door. "They won't. They had a very wholesome dinner. Of course, Noah refused to finish his meal, so he will be going to bed hungry." She held up a finger. "Do *not* feed him. He needs to learn."

Learn what? That his mother is a cold bitch? Jane was beginning to think she might have principles. *Starving a kid because he wouldn't finish his lame dinner? Disgusting.* But then Mrs. Harker opened her wallet. It was flush with cash. All the colors of the Canadian rainbow — including lots of red fifties.

Jane smiled at Mrs. Harker, hating herself a little. "They gotta learn," she said.

But instead of paying Jane up front, Mrs. Harker handed Jane a business card. It had all of the woman's contact information, even her Twitter account. "In case you need to reach me." Before Jane could touch it, Mrs. Harker gave Jane a hard stare. "Emergencies only. I do not want to field any calls about Noah complaining that he's hungry."

Jane nodded. "You won't."

"I have a very important work event this evening and I *cannot* be interrupted. Your reference said you are very qualified and I'm interpreting that to mean you can manage three children for three hours. They should certainly be in bed and asleep by the time I return." She skimmed through the cash in her still open wallet. "Three hours at $25 dollars an hour will earn you…" Mrs. Harker sighed. "Let's call it an even hundred, shall we?"

Jane's eyes bulged. Her body stiffened, as every ounce of reason told her not to jump for joy. "Sounds good."

"Good. Now let me introduce you."

Again Mrs. Harker beckoned her to follow back to the foyer, and Jane obeyed. *For a hundred bucks? She can put a goddamn leash on me.*

"Children!" Mrs. Harker clapped her hands. The children popped up. The youngest one, a little girl with blonde pigtails peered down the steps. "Come meet your sitter for the evening."

They bounded down the stairs one by one, from youngest to oldest.

"Hi," Jane said with a small wave.

"Jane, these are the children: Emma, Noah, and Olivia — the oldest. Children, meet Jane. You are to listen to her and follow all the rules. If you cannot do that, she will report back to me. Understood?"

"Yes, Mom."

"Remember, I don't want any interruptions this evening. If I get even one phone call that is less than excessive bleeding or compound fractures, I will be *very* unhappy."

"Yes, Mom."

With a flick of her wrist, she dismissed the children.

They scattered in different directions, but all three ended up in the living room on Jane's left, perched on an L-shaped couch. They giggled and whispered to each other.

Mrs. Harker reached into her wallet one last time before zipping it up and stuffing it into a Marc Jacobs bag that sat on an antique side table. She gave Jane a list of instructions and rules written on a folded piece of loose leaf. Jane skimmed it over.

"Very simple," Mrs. Harker said. "I already went over these, but in case you or the children need a reminder, it's all there."

Jane scanned it. Her mind was blank. *What had she told me about again?* No snacks. Bed by 7:30. Don't play with the Ouija board. No making a mess. Quiet activities until bedtime.

"Wait — *Ouija board?*"

CHAPTER 5

Mrs. Harker sighed again, turning to face Jane as she slipped on her coat. "Yes — haven't I explained that already? Oh, well." She lowered her voice and spoke slowly. "The children found a Ouija board in our games library, but I feel it's not appropriate for children to play with objects that bring out the worst in their imagination."

"Yeah, for sure." Jane thought about all the times she had played with a stupid Ouija board and scared the shit out of her friends. It was as fake as an alien autopsy or anything her uncle posted on Facebook. "No Ouija boards, got it."

Mrs. Harker picked up her bag and opened the door. "They may ask about it. In fact, they've been hounding me all week to play with it. I finally had to put it away on a high shelf and tell them it's forbidden, but they just can't seem to move on."

Jane was no expert on kids, but she knew herself. *You said it was forbidden.* Whenever someone said something was forbidden, then she *had* to try it.

Before she left, Mrs. Harker asked, "Can I trust you?"

"Y-yes?"

"My children can be challenging and strong-willed. They will do whatever it takes to get under your skin. Do *not* let them run roughshod over you. I trust that a babysitter with your qualifications can handle them."

"Of course," Jane said, lying to Mrs. Harker and herself.

But Mrs. Harker seemed to have bought it. She made a *hmm* sound and thanked Jane. Then without saying goodbye to the kids, she left.

As soon as Jane was alone with the kids, her heart started pounding. *Oh, shit. What do I do?* She forced herself to walk into the living room. Little Emma stood on the couch sucking her finger. Jane glanced at the list, remembering a rule. She pointed at Emma.

"No sucking your finger," she said.

Emma popped the finger out of her mouth and flopped down next to her big sister.

"Are you really the babysitter?" asked Olivia. She had long, shiny black hair and big dark eyes — and one leg propped up on the back of the couch. Another rule broken.

Damn, Mrs. H is thorough. "Legs down."

Olivia rolled her eyes but put her leg down.

Jane felt like an asshole. She crumpled up the paper

and stuffed it in her pocket. "Okay, I'm sorry. This isn't me, okay? I'm not a rule Nazi. Can we just hang out and have fun?"

"You said 'okay' twice," noted Olivia. Jane couldn't tell if she was correcting her or just making an annoying observation.

"What's a Nazi?" asked Emma.

"Uhhh…"

It's going to be a long night.

"It's a bad man," Olivia explained to her sister.

Emma trembled. "Bad man?"

"Yeah, and they're making a comeback. Right, Jane?"

"They're coming back?" Emma covered her face, peeking out between her fingers.

Jane was at a loss for words. "Uh, it's complicated…"

Noah hopped off the couch and marched up to Jane. He gave her jacket a tug, looking up at her from under a thick bowl cut. "Are you really going to tell on us to Mom?"

Jane smiled and gave him a wink. "Don't worry. I ain't no rat."

His frown turned into a beaming smile, and he swiftly kicked Jane in the shin before skipping away.

Fucker hobbled me! She dropped to one knee. "Holy sh—" She caught her tongue as little Emma hugged herself. Her wide eyes recorded everything being said.

"Are you going to let him do that?" Olivia asked.

Jane rubbed her shin. It was definitely going to be a long night.

She found herself a spot on the couch, hoping for a second to think. The two sisters jumped on the cushions and hurled themselves to the floor. Each time, the little one hurt herself and came balling to Jane, who patted her back and sent her back to her sister. Meanwhile Noah wandered in and out of the kitchen, caterwauling for a snack.

Jane had only been in the house for twenty minutes.

"Sorry, dude," she said. "Your mom said no snacks. Why didn't you eat your dinner?"

He scowled, crossing his arms dramatically. "I don't like green bean salad," he harrumphed. "I *hate* green beans."

"He hates green beans," repeated Olivia, bouncing up and down on the couch.

"Green beans are Nazis!" squealed Emma as she crashed down onto a pillow.

Noah rubbed his tummy. Anger wasn't getting him anywhere. He knelt at Jane's feet and stared up at her with big, wet eyes. "I'm *so* hungry."

His sisters paused to listen. If Noah's tactic worked, surely they would be entitled to the same benefits. Snacks were at stake, and it was likely the sisters didn't enjoy their dinner either. Noah was just more vocal about it.

"I wanna snack."

Me too, thought Jane. If she knew anything about baking, she would have tried to whip up something, but she didn't even know how to turn the oven on. *Maybe Mrs. Harker keeps one of those cake-in-a-mug boxes around.* With one of those, Jane could make a mean microwave cake.

That wasn't the point. She didn't want to let Mrs. Harker down. A hundred dollars was on the line. But then, if she didn't think of something to get this little monster out of her face, she was going to flip out and run off down the street, praying for a semi to plow her down.

"I'm hungry!"

Tears dribbled down the boy's chubby red cheeks. Deep, furious lines cut around his mouth, dragging into a perfect U shape. A grinding whine came out of him, building rapidly to a howler monkey scream. He pounded his fists against his thighs before throwing himself on the floor. His arms and legs attacked the carpet and kicked the coffee table.

"Holy shhh—" Jane knelt down, afraid to touch him lest he inadvertently punch her in the face. "Hey, buddy. You gotta stop—"

"He's not going to stop," said Olivia.

"He wants a snack," said Emma, competing with her sister for the title of Captain Obvious.

"Yeah, I get it," said Jane, leaning back. She pulled out her phone and the slip of paper with Mrs. Harker's contact info. But she hesitated. Was this really an emergency?

Hell, yeah. The dumb kid won't stop. He's going to give himself a stroke.

But Mrs. Harker only wanted to hear from Jane if something was broken or bleeding. Not if one of her brats transformed into a mega brat. And if she had to come home early, Jane's big payday would be cut in half and she wouldn't be hired again. She was sure of it. She had to make a good impression, or this sweet gig would be a one-time deal.

She put the phone away and stood up. "Okay. Chill, dude."

Silence settled over the room. The children wondered, *What is the babysitter going to do?*

Noah picked himself up. He blinked away his last few tears and started to smile.

The children followed Jane into the kitchen. First she opened the fridge. None of the rows of leafy greens and bottled water had miraculously transformed into anything tasty.

As she dug around, wishing for a tray of cupcakes or even a goddamn juice box to appear, the fridge chimed.

"That means you have to close the door," Olivia said. "You're letting the cold out."

"Global warning!" yelped Emma.

"Global *warming*," Olivia corrected.

"Christ," Jane muttered, closing the door.

"Are we going to eat something?" asked Noah. "I'm so hungry."

"Mom said we can't have any snacks," Olivia said, contradicting the vibe they were all giving off.

Jane sighed. Then she knelt down, having seen something on one of those psycho nanny shows about getting down on the kid's level and giving it to them straight. "Your mom said no snacks," she began. A cacophony of whines bubbled up from each of them. "Okay, shut up a second. Just listen. Your mom said no snacks, but I think you've all been so good that you should get snacks."

"Yeah!" agreed Emma.

"So I'll find you something, but you guys can't tell your mom."

The kids looked between each other, trying to figure out if not telling their mom would be smart or not.

Jane opened the pantry. *Hope to god there's something in here these monsters will eat.*

She jammed her body between them and the food and reached for the light switch. That's how big the pantry was — it had its own goddamn light switch.

A white glow filled the space, lighting up the canisters of flour, sugar, and cornstarch, boxes of raisins (the devil's Halloween candy), and jars of natural peanut butter. Unfortunately, Jane quickly realized there were no fun foods — just ingredients to make food, which she was not skilled to do.

Shit. "Okay, so—" *Wait. Don't tell them yet. They're gonna freak out. Think of something.*

She thought about her mom baking cookies at Christmastime and her grandmother's fresh bread at Thanksgiving.

Think harder.

She thought about being the child of a single parent who struggled to get by and still give her daughter a normal life. She thought about lazy Saturday mornings when her mom didn't have to run off to work or finish homework for nursing school. Her mom would put on a Disney movie and make—

Ah-ha!

"You kids ever eat ants on a log?"

CHAPTER 6

The children sat around the table with Jane at the head. The only sound was the occasional giggle and the crunching of celery. Jane hated celery, but it was the perfect vehicle for getting the peanut butter and raisins into her mouth. And it reminded her of her mom, who she was going to hug as soon as she saw her.

After they finished and their bellies were full, Olivia leaned back in her chair and declared, "I'm bored." This brought on echoes of the same sentiment from Noah and Emma. Jane slyly noted the time on the stove. She still had another hour before bedtime and another two hours before Mrs. Harker came home. She doubted she could handle a boredom-induced meltdown.

"Lemme think of something," she said, pulling out her phone to call Lily.

Lily answered immediately. "Everything okay?"

Behind her, the kids were whining and chanting their boredom. "Oh, yeah, totally. I just, uh, what do I do if they're bored?"

Lily laughed. *"They're bored?* That's easy! You just play with them."

Jane didn't want to play. She hadn't played anything other than video games in nine years. "Like what?"

"I don't know," said Lily, as a kid on her end started crying. "I have to go. You'll think of something."

She hung up and Jane was alone with the Harker children once again. *Thanks a lot, Lil.*

"So you guys have Nintendo?" she asked, looking around the room. For the first time, she realized there was no TV. Not hidden in a cabinet, not hung up above the fireplace. No screen that rolled down at one end of the room with a project on the other side. If there was no TV, there was no Nintendo.

"No," said Olivia. "We're not allowed to play video games."

"I'm bored," Noah reminded her and kicked Emma.

Emma howled. Jane pulled Noah away. "Hey, dude — that's your sister. Not cool."

"She's boring too!" he argued weakly. "And you suck. I'm gonna tell my mom you suck."

"Oh, yeah?" Jane's tone implied she didn't care, but the I'm-gonna-tell-on-you tactic worked wonders. "See if I care."

He grumbled, crossing his arms.

Emma reached out for a hug and Jane scooped her up.

She smelled like peanut butter and her hands stuck to Jane's shirt. *Ewwww.* But the girl was so little and cute. "It's okay," she said softly, patting her back. She looked at the other two staring back at her. "No TV... So what do you guys do for fun?"

"We play games," said Olivia.

* * *

Olivia's long, skinny arm reached into the pitch-black basement, feeling along the wall for the light switch. Jane held Emma in her arms and Noah stood at her side, staring down into the abyss. As the lights came on, Jane was surprised. It was unlike any basement she had ever hung out in. Even Lily's folks still had a roughed-in space they kept squabbling about finishing.

The Harkers' basement was, without a doubt, nicer than Jane's entire house. It was well-lit with pot lights and a few windows, and warm with lush beige carpet and taupe paint on the walls. Someone had neatly stencilled "Live Love Laugh" in between watercolour paintings of koi fish.

A U-shaped leather couch wrapped around a coffee table. On a sideboard against the wall sat a fishbowl where a tiny golden fish flitted around inside. There was no TV, but one hell of a sound system — and a record player with a bitchin' collection of vinyl. At the foot of the stairs, Jane set Emma down and ran over to check it out.

Alice Cooper, Iron Maiden, Black Sabbath, Led

Zeppelin, Rolling Stones — all of Jane's favourites. "Holy shit!" She pulled one out, drooling over the cover art, when buzzkill Olivia announced, "We're not allowed to touch those."

Jane groaned. "Music is meant to be played. You can't just leave them here collecting dust."

Olivia crossed her arms. "Those belong to Daddy."

"He's coming to get them," said Noah.

Jane slid the record back in and stepped away from the collection. "Are your parents ... separated?"

The three kids nodded, and Olivia spoke. "He and Mom fought a lot. So we made them get a divorce."

"Sure, okay," Jane muttered. She stared longingly at the collection. "Your dad has great taste."

"Daddy is a raging asshole," said Olivia. "I know I'm not allowed to swear, but it's true."

When Jane finally turned away from the collection, she noticed a shelving unit (cupboards on the bottom with shelves on top) built into the crawlspace under the stairs. As with the fridge, every shelf was fully loaded. The Harkers lived in a clean and organized home, but they had a lot of stuff — including every board game imaginable.

"Wow," she said, when Noah flicked on another light that lit up the boxes.

"Yeah," agreed Noah, opening one of the cupboards and browsing. Or was he looking for something? The cupboard door didn't stay open long before he pulled open the next one, pushing boxes around as he looked inside.

"It's not in there." Olivia slammed one of the doors. It

narrowly missed his little fingers.

"What're you looking for?" Jane asked.

"Nothing," they said in unison.

"They want the bad board," said Emma, sucking her thumb.

Olivia sighed and yanked her sister's hand out of her mouth. To Jane, she said, "Aren't you supposed to be the babysitter? No sucking the thumb — it's one of the rules."

Jane scrambled to review the list again. Sure enough: *Do not let the children suck on their thumbs or fingers, especially Emma. Noah occasionally regresses to sucking his finger, so be vigilant.* "Right, sorry. No thumb sucking."

Arms crossed, Emma pouted.

She checked the time on her phone. Bedtime couldn't come soon enough. "Just pick a game, okay? A short one."

She collapsed on the couch and waited for them. They hemmed and hawed and bickered and whispered. They pointed up and glanced back at Jane, and then chattered among themselves.

As she waited, she got a text. From Nate. "What the shit?" she muttered, looking over her shoulder.

Hey. What're you doing?

She was so stunned, her thumbs couldn't connect with her brain fast enough and she had to delete a bunch of scrambled letters before she could form the proper words.

Nothing. What's up?

He sent a smiley emoji. *Sorry I couldn't take you home*

the other day. I promised Troy.

How was yoga? she asked, adding, *;)*

At the exact moment, he sent, *You want to come over?*

Butterflies in her stomach sprang to life and danced around. She flipped over to her last conversation with Lily and was about to ask what she should do, when she remembered Lily's major crush on Nate. She flipped back to their conversation just as he sent another message on the heels of the previous one.

I'm having some friends over for a movie night. Would like to see you again.

Her face warmed and her fingers were moist from gripping the phone. *Sure*, she sent back too quickly. The three Harker children stood in front of her holding a black box.

It was the goddamn Ouija board.

Nate fired back his address. *It's in Sunshine Falls. If you get lost, I can come pick you up.*

Then Lily sent a text. *Umm. Nate Crawford just asked me for your number.*

Adding separately, *What's that about?*

Jane had a million questions, but she couldn't do a thing with the children standing in front of her, waiting to play a stupid game.

"No, pick another one," she said, trying to buy more time. She had to explain to Nate that she was stuck babysitting and explain to Lily that she wasn't a home-wrecker. Sure, she wanted to go to Nate's house and hang out and watch movies with the popular kids, but not if Lily was going to be mad at her.

"We want this one," said Olivia.

Jane dramatically lowered her phone and forced a grin. "Oh, Olivia, you little rule-breaker you. You know your mom said no Ouija boards. Off limits. Pick another one."

Olivia's face was stony. "This is the one we want."

"No."

Emma erupted into a crying fit, throwing her body down and kicking her feet. Noah jumped up on the coffee table and screamed in Jane's face, spit flying at her. Olivia held her ground, shoving the box at Jane, who felt like she was falling back into the time before she doled out snacks. *What is happening? Didn't I just fix you brats?*

She raised her phone to text Lily. *What do I do if they go ape shit?* But Olivia snatched it from her. Jane bolted upright. "Give it back."

Smirking, Olivia dance-stepped to avoid Jane's grabbing, desperate hands. Jane dashed off the couch and Olivia ran across the room to the fishbowl. Pinching the phone between her thumb and forefinger, Olivia dangled it over the unsuspecting goldfish, who burped a tiny bubble and swam around its little castle.

CHAPTER 7

Jane's breath caught. "Don't you fucking dare."

"No swearing!" shouted Emma, who had shut off the waterworks as effortlessly as her brother.

"Shut up!" Jane snapped.

Emma burst into tears again, covering her face and running into Noah's arms.

Jane couldn't deal with that right now. She took a slow, steady step toward Olivia, who dipped the phone into the bowl. One wrong move and she could drop it. If Jane couldn't convince her to hand it over, she hoped it crushed their stupid fish.

Without her phone to ask Lily for help, Jane had no idea what to do. She wasn't prepared for this. Lily was right — she needed the babysitting course. Maybe she could have learned what to do when bratty children hold her phone hostage. She couldn't even call Mrs. Harker to tap out and say, *I'm not qualified to watch your kids. I'm a fucking phony-ass bitch. Keep your money — this shit isn't worth it. I'll get a job at A&W. I'll even work at KFC and smell like grease every fucking day.*

"You want this back?" the girl asked.

Jane clutched her head as she knelt before the most powerful ten-year-old in the world. "Yes."

"What'll you do for it?"

I won't throttle your scrawny neck. "What do you want?"

"We want to have fun. We want to play with the Ouija board."

"You mom said—"

Olivia rolled her eyes in a way that hinted at the insufferable teenager she was going to be one day. "We *know* what she said. *We don't care.* We want to play the game."

Jane's gut told her they had already broken one rule too many. *But my phone...* She wasn't likely to get another babysitting job after this mess and saving up her pathetic allowance to buy a phone would take forever, and there was no way in hell her mom was going to run out and buy her a new one.

"Can't we play another game? I think this one's too advanced for you kids."

"This is the game we want to play!" yelled Noah.

"Play it!" shrieked Emma.

"Trust us, Jane," said Olivia. "It's fun. You'll see."

Fuming, Jane picked up the box and slammed it down

on the floor. "Fine." She pulled off the lid and flung it aside as the children gathered.

She spied Olivia holding her phone behind her back. Anger pounded in Jane's head. *What the hell do I care? If Mrs. Harker didn't want her kids playing with the stupid thing, she should've hidden it better.* She set the board down in the middle of a circle they formed with their bodies and set the planchette aside. Olivia reached for it and Jane snapped at her. "Wait."

Olivia recoiled, glaring at the babysitter.

"Do you even know how to play this thing?" she asked.

"Better than you," replied Olivia. "Here, we'll show you." She took the planchette and set it on the board. The other children leaned in and placed their fingers on it, next to Olivia's. "Put your fingers here."

Rolling her eyes, Jane followed along. "Fine."

"No more talking," Olivia stated. "I'll ask the questions."

"Aww," whined Emma.

Noah shushed her and then Olivia continued. "Hello. We're here. Are you there?"

Jane wondered who they were talking to. Did they already have a storyline they were following? Or had they actually made contact with a spirit on the other side?

That's bullshit, she decided. There were no such things as ghosts and spirits. Just three dumb kids playing make-believe and trying to scare each other. "What's so great about this game anyway?" she muttered, not expecting anyone to answer.

The planchette jerked across the board, then slid to different letters. It didn't feel like three children trying to prank her; it felt like someone else was in charge.

NEW FRIEND.

"This is Jane," introduced Olivia. "She's our sitter. Say hello, Jane."

"To what?" she asked, puzzled.

The planchette moved again.

ZED.

The children leaned in, beaming and exchanging bright-eyed looks. Jane didn't like any of it. The knot in her stomach tightened. "Look, this is fun and all, but your mom doesn't want you doing this, so let's pack it up, shall we?"

NO, the board replied.

Jane frowned. "You guys. You know this is bullshit, right? The box says Parker Bros. Just like Monopoly. You'll have as much luck talking to the Monopoly Man. This isn't real."

I AM REAL.

"See?" said Olivia. "We play with Zed all the time. He's very real."

"And he's fun!" said Emma. "He gives us anything we want!"

"Oh, yeah? Like what?"

"My fish," said Emma. "And my Pretty Party playsets."

"She has *all* of them," said Noah, rolling his eyes.

"Your mom and dad probably got you those," said Jane. She flicked the light wooden board. "This is just painted cardboard."

MAKE A WISH.

Make a wish? Jane looked around at their finished basement and fine furnishings, the clean clothes on their backs. The children had everything they could ever wish for. They were privileged. They had money. Whatever they wished for — *Pretty Party playsets* — could easily be acquired without the intervention of a spirit board.

Her phone buzzed from its secure spot behind Olivia. Nate and his friends were waiting.

She let out a breath. *What the hell?* "I wish I was at Nate's house."

The children giggled. The lights flickered off and on. *Some sort of trick*, she thought. And then the doorbell rang. The ball of stress in her stomach dropped down to her bowel. *None of this Ouija board shit is real and the doorbell is just a coincidence.*

"Answer it!" yelled Noah, startling her.

"Answer it, Jane," pressed Olivia.

Jane got up, pushing the board into Olivia's lap. As she plodded past them, she snatched her phone back and marched up the steps. "That's enough," she called over her shoulder. "Put the game away and go to bed."

The children groaned, watching Jane go upstairs alone. *Fine. Leave* me *to answer the demon you little jerks summoned.*

She wished at least one of them had come with her.

She didn't want to answer the door alone. She never even answered the door at home. Instead, she would creep up to the peephole and spy on the delivery driver or census worker standing on the front step. Even at seventeen, Jane religiously practiced the rules of "stranger danger."

The doorbell rang again. A dark shape flitted by the blurred glass window. *It's Zed.*

No, stupid. Zed's not real. Wishes aren't real. It's just—

She opened the door and—

Stepped across the threshold into another house.

This one had warm wooden floors and a narrow staircase that curved upward. Lights were on in every room. Music and voices blasted from the basement. A girl snorted laughter. Video games drowned out other conversations.

Nate held the door open with a surprised grin. "Hey, you made it."

CHAPTER 8

The next morning, Jane woke up with a throbbing headache. Her phone's alarm buzzed underneath her pillow, but it felt like a jackhammer pounding against her skull. She licked the corner of her dry mouth and answered the phone.

"Ugh?" she grunted.

"Good morning," said a stern voice. "Am I speaking to Jane?"

"Uh, yeah." She sat up, sweeping her hair out of her face. Strands stuck to her sweaty forward and her eyes were crusted shut.

"This is Bree Harker."

The name shot ice up Jane's spine. She scrambled to get up, willing her brain to start working because she was going to have to explain why she ditched Mrs. Harker's kids to hang out with Nate.

Once she had left those brats behind, she had the best night of her life.

Nate gave her a tour of his parents' fancy house and introduced her to all his popular, cool friends (even though Jane had been going to school with them since kindergarten). They drank beers and ate pizza and played video games.

At one point, someone dimmed the lights and all the couples started making out. Nate and Jane slipped away to sit on the basement steps where they talked all through the night. He reached over and took her hand in his, and she completely forgot about Lily and the children and Mrs. Harker.

"Mrs. Harker! I'm so—"

"You left in such a hurry last night that I was unable to pay you," she said. "Would you be able to return to the house today?"

Jane didn't remember seeing Mrs. Harker at the end of the night. Or pedalling home. Or anything other than the warmth of Nate's hands and the way they sat closely on the stairs, talking about nothing in particular.

She jumped out of bed — only to find out that she wore the same clothes from the night before, except they were damp from sweat. She changed into a clean t-shirt and hoodie as she ran through the house.

Her mom was still at the hospital, so Jane didn't have to face an interrogation about her night. A small blessing because she didn't know how to explain anything at the moment.

The rusty bike laid on the lawn, waiting for her. She got on and pedalled back to Sunshine Falls.

At the Harker house, she dumped the bike and climbed up the steps. Olivia answered, smirking. "Welcome back."

"What the hell happened?" Jane asked in a hushed voice. Her eyes darted around for any sign of Mrs. Harker. "What did you guys do to me?"

"Nothing," said Olivia. "It was all Zed."

"You made him up," she said. "He isn't real."

"No, *we summoned him* and he came to play. When we play with him, he makes wishes come true."

"Bullshit," said Jane, completely forgetting she was supposed to watch her tongue around the child. But Olivia didn't act like a child; she was more like a snarky adult trapped in a child's body. "You're messing with me. You're lying…"

Olivia clenched her small fists and stuck out her chin. *"I'm not lying.* I can prove it."

"Olivia?" called Mrs. Harker from somewhere within the house. "Who are you talking to?"

"The babysitter."

Mrs. Harker's heels clacked down the hallway as she adjusted one of her pearl earrings. She looked Jane up and down, retrieving her bag from the table. She rooted around inside and then sighed.

"My apologies," she said. "My wallet is missing. One moment." Her phone began to ring and when she checked the screen, she let out another loud sigh. "Never a moment's peace... Jane, would you mind waiting a bit longer?" She showed Jane her screen, as if the name on it meant anything to anyone other than Mrs. Harker. "Work never ends."

All work and no play... Jane thought mindlessly.

Olivia smiled up at her mom as the woman stormed off. "Mommy, can Jane come in and play?"

Mrs. Harker gave them a dismissive wave and disappeared into the adjacent room. Olivia grabbed Jane's sleeve, pulling her inside.

"I'm not here to play," said Jane. "I just want my money."

"Zed can give you more. And not just money either."

Jane shook her head, letting the child lead her back down to the basement. Emma and Noah sat around the coffee table, watching the stairs. When they saw that it was only their sister with the babysitter, they relaxed. Noah slid the Ouija board out from under the couch.

"Took ya long enough," he said.

"Jane doesn't believe us," Olivia said.

"Believe what? I don't even know what's going on," she said.

"You wished to go to a boy's house and then you did," said Olivia. "Noah wished to know how to drive. Emma wished for a fish." She snapped her fingers and pointed to the goldfish. "Zed made it happen."

"And to be a princess!" Emma added, pointing to the cheap plastic tiara on her head.

Jane snickered. "Okay, sure."

"That's right," said Olivia, reaching into the back pocket of her jeans to pull out folded pieces of paper. She handed it to Jane.

Jane pried the sticky pages apart. She didn't know what she was seeing — she couldn't understand the dense legalese, but a few choice phrases leapt out at her. *By royal designation... Emma Violet Harker, fifth in line... Will hereby be known as Princess of...* Some European country Jane had never heard of.

Her face crumpled up and she handed the papers back. "Anyone could fake this. It's called Photoshop."

"It's real," said Noah.

"And what did you wish for?" she asked Olivia. "Queen?"

"No," she replied. "Something much more important."

"She wished for Mom and Dad to get divorced," said Noah.

Jane frowned. "Why the hell would you wish for something like that?"

"Because my parents don't love each other, but neither had the guts to leave," she said. "They just kept fighting and fighting, and it was upsetting Emma. And Noah started wetting the bed again."

"Hey!" he cried.

"Something had to be done. So I asked Zed to end it, and he did. And you asked to go to a boy's house, and he made that happen too. He must really like you, because he also made my mom think you were here all night."

"You weren't," said Noah.

"You were at a boy's house!" Emma grinned and clapped her hands. "Did you kiss him?"

"Yuck," said Noah.

Jane held up her hands, trying to get a handle on this conversation. "I don't know what this is all about, but I know wishes don't come true and Ouija boards don't grant them. So if you did something or—" But what could they have done? "I probably just fell asleep or something."

She checked her phone. A text from Nate: *Nice seeing you last night. Can we do it again?*

"It wasn't a dream," said Olivia. "It was Zed. And if you come back again and play with us, he'll grant you more wishes. Anything at all."

Jane stared at the board between the two younger children. They mindlessly pushed the planchette back and forth as they listened to Jane and their big sister.

"I don't think I'm gonna come back," she said. "This is just too weird."

"Wish for something else then," said Olivia, who sat down at the board and placed her fingers on the planchette. "You'll see."

Mrs. Harker's heels clacked around on the floor above. She called out for the children, and the sound of her voice should have sent them scrambling to hide their forbidden game, but they all sat so eerily still. Their wide eyes focused on Jane.

Jane plopped down across from Olivia. "Fine," she muttered. "What do I do?"

"Put your hands on the pointer and say hello."

Jane touched the cool plastic, her fingers bumping against Noah's. "Hello."

WELCOME BACK.

"So what, I just make another wish?"

YES.

She scoffed. "Okay, then..." She thought hard about something that would be difficult for the children to fake. Perhaps they had drugged her with something from their mother's medicine cabinet, and she dreamt being at Nate's.

But Nate had texted her; they couldn't fake that.

She leaned in, staring down Olivia, and said, "I wish for a car. A beautiful blue Mustang. If you're so good at wishes, you'll know exactly the one I'm thinking of."

This time, the lights didn't flicker and the children didn't laugh. Mrs. Harker's voice cut the tension between their little group. "Jane? Children? Are you down there?"

The doorbell rang.

Jane jumped up. She raced up the stairs as Mrs. Harker answered the door. Feeling dizzy, Jane placed a hand against the wall to steady herself. She remembered seeing Nate on the other side. He had been as surprised to see her as she was to see him. What was going to be on the other side this time?

Zed.

Mrs. Harker opened the door as Jane stumbled toward her. "No, don't—"

But the only person on the other side was the FedEx guy holding a package. They both looked at Jane, pale and sweating, jaw slack.

"Are you alright?" She kept one eye on Jane as she signed for the package.

"What's in the box?" Jane asked, inching forward. Pins and needles ran through her limbs. She grabbed onto the staircase railing. *Is the car in there? Pink slips? A key? Was it possible?*

Could Zed be real?

"It's for my work, not that it's any of your business," replied Mrs. Harker, dismissing the delivery guy. She took the box into her office. "Your payment is on the table. You'll have to excuse me — I have to attend to this call."

Jane retrieved the cash, not bothering to count it. She stuffed it into her pocket, lingering near the door. If a Mustang magically appeared in Mrs. Harker's package, she would have said something by now.

So Jane muttered a thanks and let herself out. As the FedEx van pulled away and cleared the street, she froze.

Parked across from the Harker house was a hot blue 1999 Mustang.

No way...

And in her hand, the key appeared.

CHAPTER 9

Three weeks later...

Another Saturday night, another weekend lost to babysitting. At least this time, Jane travelled in style. The blue Mustang was a dream come true, but I was also too good to be true and difficult to explain to Lily.

"It's got that new car smell," Lily noted, touching the dashboard and opening the glovebox. "But there's no way your mom bought you a new car."

"She didn't," said Jane, telling the truth. The rest of her story was bunk. "Since I'm sitting so much, she thought I needed a more reliable vehicle and so we worked out a payment plan."

"Still seems like a lot of money to spend on a car to get you to and from Sunshine," said Lily.

"Relax," said Jane. "You get to enjoy the ride too."

"I know, but..."

"But what?"

"Just seems weird, you know?"

Jane knew, but she shook her head as she pulled up to a two-storey brick house on a tree-lined street. "I *don't* know. It's just a car."

"It's your dream car," said Lily, grabbing the handle.

"So? Lots of teens get their dream cars."

"They're usually on one of those *Super Spoiled Sweet Sixteen* shows, and their parents are rich."

Jane felt a headache coming on and she didn't want to keep going around and around about her car. Luckily, she had managed to hide her brand-new phone from Lily, as well as four dates she had been on with Nate. "There's nothing weird going on. I'm just really good at managing my cash, okay?"

"Okay, okay," said Lily, getting out. "I'm just worried you might've started ... selling drugs."

"Drugs? Oh, my god, Lil! Is that what you think of me?"

Lily put on her backpack. "I don't know what to think."

"I'm *not* selling drugs! Believe me." Another excuse came to mind. "Between my mom helping me and Mrs. Harker overpaying, I'm doing really well."

"She overpays?"

"Yeah." Jane swallowed, nodding eagerly. Too eagerly. She stopped suddenly. "She says she's so grateful to have someone watching her precious angels. All that crap, you know?"

Lily chewed her lip, considering.

"Hey, if the car makes you feel weird, I don't have to drive you." She swallowed again, her throat constricting.

Lily's eyes bugged out. "No! I like getting a ride. I just..." She sighed. "Forget it. I don't know what's wrong with me. It's your car. *I'm* the weird one."

Jane suppressed a grin. "Totally."

The two friends parted, and Jane headed for the Harker house. Running behind, thanks to Lily.

It's not like I made a deal with the devil — or have I?

She made a sharp turn into Sunshine. Her lights flashed over a huge, hulking shape in the middle of the crosswalk. She slammed on the brakes, narrowly missing the pedestrian — a large teen girl who punched the Mustang's hood.

Jane honked at the girl. Rolling down the window, she was about to spew all sorts of vile threats and expletives, but stopped short. The pedestrian wasn't just any girl. It was the Beast.

Fuck.

The Beast scowled, popping up her collar to cover her cold, red ears.

With a foot pressed on the brake pedal, Jane gripped the steering wheel. *Move.*

The Beast slowly crossed the street. Then Jane eased the car around the corner, though the engine growled at the slightest acceleration. The Beast jumped aside.

As soon as she passed by, Jane looked in the rear-view

mirror. The Beast had disappeared inside her hoodie, following behind.

She's after me, Jane fretted. *She's going to key my car.*

I wish— She caught herself. Spouting off wishes had come so naturally the last few weeks. *Be careful what you wish for.* Her mom's favourite piece of advice. *No wish. I just want to get to the Harker house.*

By the time she had parked the car and jogged up to the front door, the pounding in her head settled down. She rang the doorbell and took a deep, calming breath.

A gust of wind hit her and she turned as if bracing for a physical assault from the wicked weather. The porchlight across the street flicked on, putting a spotlight on one of the neighbours.

She blinked until she recognized the heavyset shape of the girl she had almost run over. The Beast stared at her.

She must have taken a shortcut.

Jane clutched her keys, fearing a fight was about to break out. But across the street, a woman answered the door and welcomed the Beast in. Two little kids jumped up and down, clapping their hands.

Damn, thought Jane. *Who would hire the Beast to look after kids?* She compared her own babysitting skills to what she knew about the Beast. *They probably wouldn't be able to bully her into snacks and forbidden games. And for that reason, she's probably really fucking good.*

But just knowing she was there was enough to give Jane a stomachache.

Mrs. Harker opened the door. "You're late," she

remarked haughtily, tapping her wristwatch.

"Sorry," she said.

Once she stepped inside and closed the door, and the children ushered her into the basement for their next round with Zed and the Ouija board, Jane thought up her next wish.

I wish something bad would happen to the Beast.

* * *

The next day at school, she parked by Nate's Volkswagen. He grinned. "Nice wheels. Wanna drag?"

She grinned back. "I'd blow the doors off your little roller skate."

"Guess you don't need me to rescue you from the Beast anymore, huh?"

"Nope." She shook her head as she grabbed her books and began walking toward the school with Nate. "Got my own ride now. Don't have a use for you anymore."

"I'm sure you could think of something," he teased, bumping her with his elbow.

She caught Lily's puzzled stare from across the parking lot. Her mousy friend hugged her books, waiting at the entrance. Jane said a quick goodbye to Nate and split off to meet up with Lily. Guilt twisted her stomach like a knife; she hadn't yet told her that she had been hanging out with her crush.

"Hey..." she began, trying to think of way to spin the situation.

"Did you hear?" Lily asked.

Jane followed her inside. "Uh, hear what?"

"Barbara Stanley was in a bad accident."

"Who?"

"Barbie?"

"I don't know anyone named Barbie."

Lily huffed and shook her head. "You call her the Beast, which is kinda mean, by the way."

The Beast? "What happened?"

"I heard from my mom who read it in the paper. She broke her leg in a hit-and-run on Saturday."

CHAPTER 10

It wasn't her leg, Jane discovered after rushing home at the end of the school day to find the newspaper article. (There was nothing online because the *Morganville News* was behind the times with using its website. All Jane could do until school let out was drive herself crazy by refreshing the website a million times.)

Barbara Stanley had broken her foot during an encounter with a reckless driver in the Sunshine Falls neighbourhood after a babysitting job. There was no description about the car or its driver, but Jane had a terrible sinking feeling the accident had something to do with her wish, the Mustang, and the Harker children's Ouija board.

As soon as Mrs. Harker left the house the following Saturday, the children pulled on Jane's sweater to lead her down to the basement. "I'm gonna wish for so much candy!" was one of their announcements. Little Emma gleefully danced around.

"Wait, guys," said Jane. "We have to talk about this."

The children formed a straight line and stared up at Jane with serious faces.

"What does your mom think about all this?" she asked.

"She doesn't know," said Olivia. "And she doesn't need to know."

"And as long as it's a secret, we can do whatever we want," said Noah. He rubbed his stomach. "And I want candy!"

"Super secret!" added Emma.

Jane backed up against the counter and crossed her arms. "Well, I don't feel good about this anymore. A girl from my school got in a bad accident."

Olivia tipped her head to one side, studying Jane. "We didn't wish anything bad about a girl at your school. So it must be your fault."

Jane's sweater felt too hot and itchy, her armpits clammy. "I'm not pointing fingers. I'm just saying we don't know what we're dealing with."

"It's just Zed," she replied.

"We're having fun," added Noah.

"We can't stop now."

Jane's new phone chimed. She pulled it out and read Nate's text. *Whatcha doin?*

Babysitting, she replied.

Boo.

Tell me about it.

And then the phone was out of her hand and in Noah's. "Keep away!" he shouted, dashing out of the kitchen.

"Give it back!" she screamed, running after him. Emma stuck out a foot, taking her down. Jane stared at her like she was insane. "Emma, Jesus Christ—"

Noah hollered from the living room, waving her phone around. "This is fun!"

She pushed herself up off the floor, leaving little Emma behind in the living room.

Noah bounced off every piece of furniture and then flew through the air, landing at the other entryway. He snorted, disappearing around the corner. Jane listened to his heavy footfalls leading her back to the kitchen and then downstairs.

Little shit!

"Stop stealing my phone!"

Down below in the dark, the children giggled.

"Play with us, Jane," called Olivia.

We don't need the board, she wanted to tell them. *We opened something. You opened something... It's dangerous. And it is my fault. I should have stopped you before. And we need to stop this now.*

She choked on her words.

Her shaking hands tensed on the doorframe. *I'm not going down there.* One of the children whispered, "We wish Jane would play a game with us..."

She felt weak, fearing she would soon be drawn into the dark depths of the house and forced to play with the Ouija board. But no invisible push or pull forced her to move, and she remained at the top of the stairs.

Then the kitchen lights flickered, and the doorbell rang.

Oh, no.

She was compelled to answer it, but what would she find on the other side? She went to the door and opened it and—

Nothing. The porchlight was on and her Mustang was parked on the street. Across the road, the Beast hobbled up to the neighbour's door in a bulky medical boot. She cast a dirty look in Jane's direction and Jane quickly shut the door.

What's the matter with me? Maybe I'm working too much. Maybe I'd be better off at KFC. At least I could throw hot grease at the Beast if she attacked me there. All I've got here is celery.

She returned to the kitchen and poured herself a glass of water from the tap. She held the cool glass against her head, rallying herself to go downstairs and order the little brats to bed. There was no way in hell she was going to touch that Ouija board ever again.

And then, as if she had made a wish, the three little monsters marched upstairs. The youngest two said goodnight and went straight to their rooms. Olivia stopped to return Jane's phone.

"My mom's calling you," she said solemnly, before following her siblings.

Elated to have her phone back, Jane pumped her fist as soon as the kids were out of sight. Sure enough, Mrs.

Harker's name and number flashed on her screen. She answered it, ready to quit right then and there, even if it ruined Mrs. Harker's night out.

I don't need this job anymore. I got the car. That's the whole reason I was babysitting to begin with. Now I'm just being greedy.

"Hi, Mrs. H. I—"

"A work emergency came up," said Mrs. Harker. "I'm afraid I'll be in the office a few hours longer than I hired you for. Do you think you could stay an extra three hours? I'll pay you double."

Double! Jane did the math, weighing it against her desire to quit. *Double is double! I can at least stick it out one more night.*

"Hell yeah!" The decision was easy to make without the kids around to drive her nuts. If they stayed in bed the rest of the night, she was on easy street. "I mean, yes, I can totally do that. No problem."

"I may not be home until midnight," she said. "Help yourself to anything in the fridge. Are the children in bed?"

"They just went up."

"Any problems?"

Jane was already counting and spending her money. "Nope. They've been little angels."

CHAPTER 11

While Jane helped herself to a fancy water and a celery stick loaded with peanut butter, the children gathered in Olivia's room, the de facto location for playing and conspiring against the grownups. It was where Olivia made the decision that their parents had to get divorced.

Her room had a kid-sized walk-in closet where she had spent an entire afternoon transforming it into a 10-year-old girly-girl's pink and purple war bunker.

Noah hated it (calling it the Cootie Den), but he joined his sisters nonetheless. "How much longer?"

"I'm not sure," said Olivia. Keeping the ceiling light off, she turned on a flashlight so they could give the illusion to the nosy babysitter that they were asleep in their separate rooms and not meeting surreptitiously in a closet with glitter glue on the carpet. "Jane is annoying.

All she cares about is her dumb phone."

"Just like Mom," said Noah, shaking his head.

"When are we gonna have fun?" Emma whined, pulling on her own hair.

Olivia shushed her. "We just have to be quiet and wait for Jane to go to sleep."

"He said to cut her," whispered Noah.

"Blood is yucky," said Emma.

Olivia looked around the closet. On one side was a cabinet for her clothes and stuffed animals, and on the other, a container for art supplies. She pulled on one of the stickier drawers and it lurched open. She poked around with the flashlight until she found a jar filled with rainbow-coloured gems. Grabbing a handful and three gel pens, she assigned tasks to her siblings. "We need stones with a Z on them. Write a Z," she ordered.

Noah scribbled out his Zs and glanced over at Emma with a dramatic sigh. "She's making *Ss*, Liv."

"No, I'm not!" argued Emma, who was trying really hard. "It's just upside down. See?" She flipped it over. It was still an S.

Noah sighed again, taking the gem from her. He licked his thumb to wipe off the gel ink and wrote a proper Z. "There. *That's* a Z."

"It looks the same," said Emma.

"That's 'cause you're dyslexic."

"We need a sacred item," said Olivia.

"What's sacred mean?"

"It means important."

"I know!" Emma jumped up and ran out of the closet. The other two warned her to be quiet, but Emma was already gone.

"Dumb kid," muttered Noah.

"She's only five," said Olivia. "She's too young to be dumb."

"I was dumb at five," he said.

"You're dumb now," she replied, pocketing the gems.

"Hey—"

Emma came back in, squeezing Mr. Hugs, a fluffy, stuffed Easter bunny that was half her height. "I love him *so* much."

"Does that count as sacred?" asked Noah. "A stupid rabbit?"

Olivia rubbed her chin, mimicking what their mom did when she was pretending to think. "Maybe. Is it important to you, Em?"

Emma nodded furiously. "Yes, yes, yes! Mr. Hugs is more important than anything," she gushed, squeezing and rocking the stuffed animal back and forth.

"Anything?" questioned Noah. "Even air?"

"She's *five,*" Olivia reminded him.

"It's just a stupid bunny," he said. "Why would Zed care?"

"It's sacred to *Emma*," she said. "Even if you don't care, Emma does."

"What about the babysitter?" he asked. "What do you think she cares about?"

* * *

Jane stretched out on the couch and put her feet up. Might as well get comfortable if she was going to be hanging out for a few more hours. The kids were in bed and there was no TV. All Jane had was her precious phone and a couple of downloaded games. No movies or shows to watch unless she wanted to use up her data, and if she played the games too long, she would drain her battery.

Right now, she needed her battery to let her mom know that she had picked up some overtime. After she fired off a quick text, she waited to see her mom's response, even though it was silly to wait. Her mom was working the night shift again and wouldn't check her phone until her break.

But Lily had sent her six texts. *What the hell?* Jane skimmed them. They were all about Nate and how he was going out with someone and she was heartbroken and did Jane know anything about this other woman?

Feeling sweaty all over again, Jane replied, *Don't know. I'm babysitting.*

Three blinking dots. Lily was attached to her phone. *You haven't heard anything?*

No. You?

No. Thought you might have heard something since I've seen you hanging around him and his friends. :/

Jane scrunched up her burning face. She didn't like the look of that crooked sideways emoji staring back at her. Was this a trap? Was sweet, nonconfrontational Lily trying to lure Jane out and then smash her over the head with a truth bomb?

Her thumb hesitated over the screen as she drafted a response.

It's probably just a rumour. You know what all those jerks are like.

Yeah, I guess, replied Lily. *How are your kids?*

Assholes, she texted. *One of them kicked me and another tripped me, and they stole my phone. AGAIN!*

Lily: *Hard work, lol?*

Jane chomped down on her lip. She didn't hear the kids upstairs whispering in Olivia's closet or rooting through the craft supplies, nor did she hear Emma running in and out of her room to retrieve a big stuffed bunny.

The money's good, but I think I'm done after tonight, she said. *Talk later?*

Yeah, later.

A text from Nate came in.

* * *

Olivia filled her backpack with the gems, Mr. Hugs, a few pieces of chalk, and a picture Zed had them draw during another one of his games. He had them close their eyes so he could show them how to draw a special star in a circle.

But to do that, they had to let go so he could take over.

Olivia struggled with "letting go," as Zed instructed. Much like her mom, Olivia could never shut off her brain. She was always scheming and trying to stay four steps ahead of her siblings. She couldn't reveal that she didn't know something, so she had to always be "on." But when they played with Zed, he wanted her to check out. Leave her body, so he could show them each a trick.

That was easy for young Emma and dopey Noah, but Olivia didn't know how to let go. It took a lot of coaching from Zed, and luckily he admonished the other two when they started to pick at her. Even though she kind of deserved it for all those times she acted like a superior know-it-all, Zed wouldn't allow their teasing. They were playing a game and learning; no need to be cruel.

Zed's games were meant to be fun.

Once Zed was able to get inside her head and talk to her, Olivia managed to let go. Zed quickly took over. He curled her fingers around the pencil and moved her arm in a circle. Around and around. She tittered nervously and started to return to her natural, rigid self until he rocked her back into place. She felt dizzy and silly — both of which made her anxious — but she copied Noah and laughed instead of screaming, *I don't want to let go! Don't make me!*

When Zed finished showing them what to draw, Noah and Emma thought their pictures were neat, but also kind of stupid. A pointed star in a circle? They couldn't see what Olivia saw, and what she saw, she didn't like. It was a bad symbol. Evil.

But she also wanted to do it again. She wanted to know what other games Zed had up his sleeve, because for once, she had been able to float away from the tense little world she had been born into.

Zed had a plan for that too. He could help her. Fun times for everyone, if he could just find a way to be a *real boy* again. Zed wasn't a ghost like Noah believed. He was a boy from Texas who had been playing with his parents' Ouija board when something went wrong, and he ended up stuck inside it. All he wanted was a friend.

Olivia didn't believe it at first. Her default was "trust no one," but she kept returning to the board by herself. She asked Zed questions and he told jokes and showed her tricks, like flickering the lights and ringing the doorbell.

And though she had never seen his face — he told her he had sandy blonde hair and green eyes — she started to like him. He understood her, unlike the mean kids at her school. So when he brought up the idea of breaking free, she didn't overthink it for once. If she could save Zed, he just might like her back.

Olivia adjusted the backpack as she peered down from the second-storey landing. The hallway was clear and the light was off in the kitchen. That meant Jane was either in the bathroom or the living room.

She took a step down.

Creeeak.

She eased back, waiting for the babysitter to jump out and yell at her. But Jane wasn't nosy like that.

Still, Olivia held her breath and waited. If she knew exactly where Jane was, it would be easier to slip into the kitchen and get the knife.

CHAPTER 12

Jane swallowed, checking the text from Nate. *Hey. What're you doing right now?* Seeing his name made her feel guilty for lying to Lily. She pulled her hoodie up around her head, wrapped up like a mummy.

Babysitting. What else? she replied.

She set her phone down, thinking she was going to have to either come clean with Lily or put an end to things with Nate.

The floor in the hallway creaked. She sat up, listening for the sound of tiny feet.

Her phone dinged as Nate sent a new text. *Can I come rescue you?* Adding, *Is the kid asleep? ;)*

She peered down the hallway. It was too dark to see anything, but no other creaking sounds followed. *Probably just my imagination.* She picked up her phone and replied, *I hope so. And there's three of them.*

Nate: *Whoa! Three? How do you do it?*

For the money. She added the emoji with dollars in its eyes and another one laughing, as if to shrug off that she only thought about money. It was true, but he didn't need to know that.

How late are you working?

Midnight — maybe longer.

Sucks.

Yeah, they don't even have a TV. Crazy!

Lily's suspicions were closing in, and if she saw this conversation, the truth would come out. Then Jane wouldn't have any friends.

I could come over and keep you company, Nate texted.

Jane: *It's Saturday night. I thought you cool people had parties to go to.*

Nate: *Everybody's just vaping outside.*

No TV or movies here. Sorry, she wrote back, though she badly wanted him to come over and hang out. The house's occasional creak and groan creeped her out. *It's just the house settling.* She didn't realize newer homes made so many noises. On top of that, the Beast was right across the street, plotting her revenge.

That's okay, Nate said. *I still want to see you.*

Jane threw her head back and sighed — catching sight of a small foot just outside of the living room. Someone *was* creeping around in the hall.

Just go the fuck to sleep! she wanted to scream. She fired off a quick text to Lily. *What do you do when the fuckin' brats won't sleep?*

Who? Lily asked, as Jane charged after the kid, who disappeared once again into the dark basement.

Harker kids! They're the worst! I'm gonna MURDER THEM!

"Hey!" she shouted. "Get back to bed!"

Olivia's ghostly white face appeared at the foot of the stairs. In a blink, she was gone.

"Get back here!" Jane cried.

She tore down the stairs after Olivia. Darkness swallowed her. She forgot the layout, and the walls felt too close. Olivia could have been right in front of her, but Jane couldn't see a thing.

"Olivia, time for bed," she said, reaching for the light switch on the wall. When it wasn't where it was supposed to be, panic closed in.

Her shin hit something hard — *fuck!* The coffee table! She had overcorrected. It was too dark. She needed her phone — which she had abandoned on the couch upstairs. "Shit. Olivia…"

"Hurry," said a child's hushed voice. More movements all around. Giggles followed.

All three of them were downstairs.

"Guys," she said, reaching out. She found a shelf and followed it to its edge. "It's late. You need to go to bed." More giggles, a few snickers, which made her blood boil. *"Upstairs. Right now."*

Something glowed on her left — her phone? Small, black shadow hands clutched it, floating it gently to the floor. Jane's hands eventually found the light switch and—

The Ouija board was right where they had left it, but a terrible mess surrounded it.

The three little monsters had drawn a pentagram in pink chalk and placed a stuffed bunny in the center — along with Jane's phone. Noah and Emma giggled behind their hands, but Olivia stared at Jane with an ice-cold expression. And she held a chef's knife.

"What the fuck?" Jane stepped back. "Your mom is gonna lose her shit when she sees this."

The younger ones giggled even louder.

"This isn't funny!" she shouted. "Clean this up right now!"

"No!" Noah barked.

"And put that knife down," she ordered. "You're gonna hurt somebody."

"I know," Olivia said. She lunged at Jane.

Jane dodged the knife. "What the fuck?"

She was tempted to leave the little monsters to their satanic bullshit, but if their mom came home to two dead bodies and Olivia covered in blood, Jane would be on the hook. But this was beyond her pay grade. She needed an adult.

Olivia shrieked, charging again.

"Put the knife down, Olivia! Or you're in big fucking trouble!" Jane screeched.

She ducked aside, crashing into Noah, who shouted, "I got her, Liv!" He shoved Jane back into Olivia's warpath, narrowly avoiding being stabbed himself. Olivia skidded to a stop, falling onto the stairs.

"Get off!" Jane pushed Noah back, smacking him across the face. She flinched. She hadn't meant to hurt him.

The boy dropped down and started crying.

Emma jumped up and down on the couch, yelling, "Zed! Zed! Zed!"

"Everybody, shut up!" screamed Jane.

Strangely enough, everyone did.

Jane held out her hand to Olivia. "Give me the knife."

Slumped on the stairs, Olivia simmered.

"I'm not fucking around!" Jane shouted. "Give me the fucking knife!"

Olivia got up, dragging her feet, and went to Jane. The knife dangled from her fingertips. But as soon as she was in striking distance, she swiped the knife across Jane's palm, slashing it open. Blood splattered on the carpet and Jane gasped.

Turning pale, Olivia dropped the knife.

"What the fuck is that matter with you?!" Jane screeched, squeezing her hand. Blood oozed out, and she had to resist the urge to cry for her mom and tell the little assholes to fuck off. She kicked the knife away; it spun across the floor, coming to a stop next to the bunny. Her blood streaked across the carpet.

With a sneer, Olivia glared at Jane and said, *"I wish you were dead."*

The house quaked. The foundation beneath Jane's feet

trembled. The popcorn ceiling cracked and flaked, raining drywall dust.

"The house is falling down!" cried Emma.

Olivia pressed against the wall, looking all around with wide eyes as the lights blinked off and on, off and on.

Board games rattled and fell off the shelves as the cupboard doors flew open and slammed shut. Above, the doorbell rang and rang.

Meanwhile, Jane's heartbeat throbbed in her palm. All she could do, aside from drip blood on the carpet, was watch in horror as the pink chalk pentagram burst into flames, engulfing everything within: Jane's phone, the knife, and one very flammable bunny.

"Jesus!" she cried.

The earthquaking stopped and the lights returned to normal, but Jane ran in circles looking for a fire extinguisher as the children huddled together. Finally, with no other option, she snatched the fishbowl and dumped its water over the burning rug. The fire sizzled out. Smoke curled up from the disaster zone. Jane hurled the empty bowl aside and dropped to her knees. Beside her, Emma's little goldfish flopped around, gasping for breath.

The basement was silent until the fish died. Sobbing, Emma walked over and collapsed next to Jane.

Just when it couldn't get any worse, the smoke alarm went off, splitting Jane's aching head wide open.

CHAPTER 13

Jane ordered the children to wave pillows and towels at the smoke detectors to clear the air. After a minute of strenuous flapping, the smoke dissipated and the alarm stopped. Jane picked up her burnt phone — it was deader than the fish — and decided that Mrs. Harker and her brood owed her a new phone.

I didn't earn this one to begin with, though.

She threw it onto the messy pile of board games and turned on the children. "What the hell? Are you the stupidest people in the world? You almost burned the whole house down!"

"We knew what we were doing," mumbled Noah, glancing at his big sister.

Olivia nodded, but her dark eyes stared at her feet.

Holding out her bleeding hand, Jane cocked her head at the girl. "And what about *this?*"

"We needed blood," she muttered.

"For what?"

Olivia glanced at the smoldering mess of carpet and then back down at her feet. She rubbed one socked toe over the others. "For Zed."

"For what?" Jane could barely contain her rage.

"For…"

Jane felt creepy all over. "I heard you!"

The doorbell rang. Olivia darted toward the stairs, but Jane caught her by the shoulder. "No fucking way. You're all gonna clean up this mess before your mom gets home, and then I'm gonna tell her *everything* so she kills you." She marched upstairs, pointing back at them. "Get on it — *now!*"

Once she was back on the main floor, she slammed the basement door. It felt like locking them up in a dungeon. Satisfying. But not for long. She grabbed her head — *what the fuck am I going to tell Mrs. Harker?* — and smeared blood on her cheek. *Shit.*

The doorbell rang again. Gritting her teeth, Jane stormed into the foyer. She looked and felt savage, ready to scare away whoever dared visit at this time of night.

Snarling, she threw open the door and—

"Hey." With his hands tucked into his pockets, Nate grinned — until he noticed the blood. "Is this a bad time?"

* * *

After Jane slammed the door, the children waited. No one spoke. The basement stank of smoke and foul fish water. Breaking the tension, Emma laid on the couch and wept like a Disney princess.

Noah scuffed the pentagram chalk marks with his toe. "Mom's gonna go insane."

Olivia blinked away tears. She had made her wish — why hadn't Zed made it happen? The stupid babysitter should be dead. The doorbell rang and everything!

Maybe Zed was bored of them. Bored of *her*. He probably left them to find another girl. Or maybe she didn't follow his orders correctly. *No,* she argued. *I did everything right.* Not knowing why Zed didn't kill the babysitter then and there was frustrating. Like when a teacher doesn't grade a test right away.

She knelt next to the Ouija board, swirling the planchette around. "Zed?"

Noah hovered over her shoulder. "It's over, Liv." When he gently placed his hand on her trembling shoulder, she snapped her teeth at him.

"Get offa me!"

Noah backed up.

Tears blurred her eyes as she ignored her siblings and the sound of Jane walking around upstairs. She focused on finding Zed. "Are you there?" she whispered.

After the longest minute of her life, the planchette responded with a firm pull.

YES.

"I made a wish. Did you hear?"

YES.

"Did it work?"

NO.

Olivia's lip quivered. She was never going to save Zed now. "What can I do?"

NOTHING.

"Please," she begged. The loneliness of her whole entire life came crashing down. Birthday parties without any friends. Being picked last in gym class, or any class. Having to eat in the classroom with a teacher so the other kids wouldn't pick on her. It would never get better. Unless she had Zed, she would always be a lonely loser. "Please?"

Zed didn't respond. The board was motionless, cold. A tear escaped from Olivia's eyelid, rolling down her cheek. She let go of the planchette, releasing it like it burned her skin, and furiously wiped the tear away with the back of her hand. As she shoved away from the table, the planchette moved on its own.

REMEMBER.

She clambered back to the board and put her hands on the planchette. "Get over here!" she ordered the others. They ran over. "Zed?" she asked again.

REMEMBER THE DRAWING GAME.

"Yeah?" she whispered.

LET GO.

Letting out a shaky breath, she closed her eyes and tried to relax her shoulders. But her heart was beating so fast and she couldn't stop thinking, couldn't let go no matter how much she wanted to.

"I-I can't..."

YES.

Squeezing her eyes shut, she tried. She kept her fingers on the planchette and tipped her head back. She breathed in and out, in and out. She stole a peek at her siblings. Both their little coconut heads lolled around on their limp necks. Their eyes were shut and their minds far away. That it was so easy for them made her even more anxious. It was just not going to happen for old Liv.

She sniffled, panic welling up in her throat. "Zed? It's too hard. I—"

The planchette moved. She followed each letter, pins and needles creeping up and overtaking her body.

LET GO.

"I can't!" she sobbed.

GO TO THE CIRCLE.

She got up, wiping her hands on her pajamas, and went to the pentagram. Her feet sank into the soggy carpet. "Now what?"

Emma and Noah followed, heads drooping. They looked like they were sleepwalking. But as they joined her at the circle, their movements came in herky-jerky bursts. They each grabbed one of Olivia's hands. She shivered as their cold skin touched hers.

The planchette again moved, and again no one controlled it. Olivia watched with wide eyes.

WISH GRANTED.

The chalk outline began to glow. The smell of smoke

intensified, and the carpet once again burst into flames around them. Olivia gasped. The flames settled down, contained to the outline.

"You're here," she sighed.

SOON.

Olivia's heart ached. They were so close now. Any moment Zed would be free and she could hold his hand.

Except she couldn't feel her hands. She tried to lift them, but her siblings' grips were too heavy. Nor could she feel her feet or face or—

"I can't move!" she squeaked through a stiffening jaw. *"Help! Stop"*

But she could move — or rather, something moved her. *I didn't let go,* she argued.

<*Always arguing, never letting go. I'm a little disappointed.*>

Zed was inside her head, pushing her out. She felt heavy with sleep. *No, I'm still here. You can't make me leave!*

She didn't have a choice. The possessed children circled the Ouija board for one more message.

TIME FOR FUN.

ONE MORE GAME.

No... Olivia closed her eyes as evil snuffed out her soul.

Zed's next instructions were clear.

KILL THE BABYSITTER.

CHAPTER 14

Jane perched on the kitchen counter with her hand under the sink's running water. She winced and whined as Nate did his best to distract her from the pain. Then he cleaned her wound with a kitchen rag that looked more expensive than anything in her wardrobe.

His fingers squeezed her hand gently, making butterflies flutter around in her stomach.

He gazed up at her from under his dark lashes. "It doesn't look too deep," he said.

"What're you, a doctor?" she teased.

He ripped open a big square bandage that he found while rooting through one of the upstairs bathrooms and applied it to her palm, explaining that his dad had been an EMT for a number of years before the stress burned him out. Then he took a lousy office job in the city and moved the family out to Morganville where the property tax was cheaper.

"That's how I learned first aid," he said.

"Cool," said Jane.

He smiled, looking away. "I was feeling bad about crashing your babysitting thing," he said, "but now that I know you needed me to rescue you again—"

Jane raised her eyebrows. "Excuse me? Again?"

He let go of her hand to wring out the cloth. "Yeah, again. The Beast, remember?"

Only too well. She sighed. "Okay, but how did you know I was here?"

He pulled out his phone and showed her their text exchange. Her face heated up as she realized her last two panicked messages to Lily had gone to Nate by mistake.

What do you do when the fuckin' brats won't sleep?

Nate: *Who?*

Harker kids! They're the worst! I'm gonna MURDER THEM!

Jane buried her face in the crook of her elbow. "You didn't think I was *actually* going to murder them, did you?"

He shrugged. "Naw, but I knew who you were talking about. My mom is 'Miss Social Committee.' The second we moved in, she was up and down the block introducing herself."

"Sounds ... embarrassing?"

"It was, but that's how we met the Harkers and how I knew where to find you."

Jane held her throbbing, bandaged hand against her chest. "Well, I'm fine," she said curtly. She wanted to tell him to go away, that she wasn't flattered that he came to check on her, that he wasn't the cutest boy who had ever paid her any attention. That because Lily liked him first, she was a terrible friend for seeing him behind her back.

But then he leaned in with a grin, tilting his head up to kiss her. She closed her eyes and leaned in, complicit in their affair. His lips were warm and smooth. She blushed, a shiver running through her bones.

Nate parted and touched her arm. "You okay? Want my coat?"

She shook her head. "No, it's—" She decided to tell him the truth. Let him know about Lily's feelings and break it to him gently that they shouldn't be together.

Instead, the three little monsters she was supposed to be watching started screaming like they were on fire.

Jane jumped down from the counter, pushing Nate aside. *I'm gonna fucking kill them—*

"What was that?" Nate asked.

She threw open the basement door. "You little shits are in for it this time!"

"Jane—"

She cut him off as she charged into the dark basement. The kids had turned off the lights and were once again running around in the dark. This time, she found the light switch and turned it on. Nate creeped down after her, staying close to the wall.

While a small fire fizzled out near the couch, Olivia,

Noah, and Emma stood in the middle of the pentagram holding hands.

"I told you to clean up and go to bed!" Jane yelled. "What the hell have you been doing all this time?"

The children didn't move. They stood unnaturally rigid, as if they had been bent and folded like origami, ready to spring forward at any moment.

"Waiting for you," they said, their gravelly voices in unison.

Unnerved, but still raging inside, Jane stepped forward. "That's it. I've had enough of your bullshit. And where did you leave that knife?"

Olivia held it.

Jane's eyes narrowed. "Put it down and *get the fuck upstairs.*"

She took a step back as Olivia moved forward. She didn't want them to come too close on their way upstairs. They might graze her skin, their bones snapping and crackling under their pale flesh.

Then Nate stepped in.

"Okay, everybody," he said with a tone that said he was used to speaking confidently and getting everyone's attention. "No more games—"

"We like games," they said.

"—This is a pretty big mess, but if we all work together—"

Olivia lunged at him. He let out an *oof* of hot air, doubling over. He grabbed his stomach with both hands, stumbling away from the weird little girl. Blood oozed between his fingers, slopping all over the carpet as he tried to get back.

Olivia struck again, stabbing him in the gut for the second time, twisting the blade as she withdrew it.

Nate turned to Jane, reaching out to her. He choked on his words, falling to one knee.

"Stop it!" Jane cried, afraid to get close to any of them, even poor Nate.

Olivia plunged the knife into his back, where it lodged in his spine. She kicked him off and he fell against the stairs.

"Stop it!" Jane screamed.

Nate gasped, trying to climb up. The children surrounded him. Jane moved farther and farther away. Her calf hit the coffee table, rattling the Ouija board and its planchette. She yelped at the sight of it.

I wish—

Noah grabbed a handful of Nate's hair, jerking his head back. Like an executioner, Olivia stood on the other side and cut the knife across his throat. Blood gushed down the steps. They let his head drop and watched him bleed out.

CHAPTER 15

Sobbing, Jane kept her back to the wall. She didn't dare go near the children. Something was terribly wrong with them.

They turned to look at her, devilish grins on their otherwise blank faces. They followed her every move.

"What's wrong with you?!" she screamed, patting herself down in search of her phone. "I'm calling the cops!" But her phone wasn't with her. It laid uselessly on the sofa above.

She had to get upstairs.

She took a bold step forward. The children didn't block her, but they didn't back away. As soon as she came too close, Olivia swiped the knife at her. She held the blade underhand like some child prodigy assassin.

"Get the fuck away from me!" Jane spun around, making a break for the stairs.

Noah skittered backwards, standing on Nate's back. Blocking her escape, he crouched down and hissed. Without second guessing, Jane punched him in the face. His nose crumpled and he fell back, sliding down Nate's body until he was laid out on the floor.

"Noah!" she gasped.

As much as she was through with this shit and would never babysit again (and would never, ever dream of having her own children), her heart ached when she saw Noah curl up on his side. He was just a kid, after all.

Until he raised his head and snarled.

Jane scrambled up the stairs, sobbing as she passed Nate.

The children followed, their small feet thumping after her. Jane looked over her shoulder. Olivia was on her tail; she raised her skinny arm, about to stab again. Jane grabbed the doorframe, dragging herself off the last step and sliding into the kitchen. She slipped, spinning around, and slammed the door in the child's face.

Then she collapsed against the door. "Jesus Christ."

Before she could think, before she could even catch her breath, the door banged against her. She pushed it shut, then reached up to lock it. But there was no lock.

Olivia let out a horrendous shriek. The younger children followed her lead. They began to hurl their bodies against the door, pounding against Jane's throbbing skull and howling in her ear.

"Stop it! Stop it!" she cried.

Jane wedged herself between the door and the opposite

storage closet, pushing back with all her strength. If she dared move, they would spill into the kitchen and carve her up. And if she couldn't reach her phone, she would be stuck there until Mrs. Harker came home.

Her eyes and nose burned with tears, and she couldn't even lift her hand to wipe her face just in case the children bullied the door open at that moment.

She pressed her full weight against the door, praying that some nosy neighbour would hear them or that Mrs. Harker would miraculously arrive home early or that Nate wasn't really dead.

I left him. Oh, shit. I left him down there with those—
<Demons.>
—monsters.

Oh my god. He's dead. He's fucking dead. They slit his throat. They killed him.

They're going to kill me too.

Her right palm, pressed against the crack in the door, burned icy hot. She jerked away, her palm smeared with blood — and a slice from her wrist bone to her pinkie. The wrapping Nate put on it was torn. Then she noticed the knife jabbing at her from under the door.

The door shot open and Jane kicked it closed, catching a small hand in the jamb. The child yelped, and the hand slithered back into the basement.

Jane couldn't hold them off much longer. She had to run for it. But first she needed something to brace the door, so she could get a head start. To where — she had no fucking clue.

Home... I wanna go home...

With a foot propped against the basement door, she elbowed open the storage closet and blindly reached behind for anything. A broom, a Swiffer, and assorted other cleaning tools tumbled out, one after the other. Unfortunately, they landed away from her.

She slumped back down, both legs holding off the children, and then stretched for the broom handle. The children shoved, her fingers pushed the handle away. It rolled in the opposite direction, just far enough that she would have to give up holding the door shut to grab it.

Gritting her teeth, she reached as far as she could. Her muscles pulled and strained, and she had the vaguest thought about Troy Manders and his goddamn yoga. She strained a muscle but managed to clasp the broom and swing it toward the door, swatting away another little hand that slipped out. Blood-sticky fingers curled around the door as it slammed shut.

Jane shoved her shoulder against it and stuck the handle under the doorknob. It wasn't perfect and it wouldn't hold for long, but it jammed up the door so that all that the children could do was turn the knob back and forth until they could jimmy the broom loose.

She sprang to her feet and rushed through the living room. She scooped up her phone and grabbed her jacket. She barely had slipped her feet into her shoes when the broom fell with a clatter and the basement door creaked open.

Without a second thought, Jane ran out the front door.

***

Digging through her pockets for her car keys, Jane came up empty handed. *Fuck!* And when she looked up, the Mustang was gone. In its place was her rusty old bicycle. *What the fuck?*

Owning the Mustang began to feel like a dream. Had it been real? Or had she been cycling around on a shitty bike bragging about her "Mustang," and therefore, losing her goddamn mind?

She didn't have time to question her reality — the children were coming.

So she picked up the bike and with a running start, jumped on as the Harker children tore out of the house. Their little bodies made jerky, spider-like movements, darting across the lawn.

A bright light flashed over them. Jane looked forward in time to see a car coming at her. The driver laid on his horn. Jane swerved aside, braking suddenly to cover her face.

Don't hit me!

The car veered around.

An idea hit her instead — *help!*

The car zipped past as she frantically waved her arms. *"Help! Please! Stop!"*

But the driver didn't stop. Jane steered around to follow the car just as Noah spider-stepped into the street. His feet made soft padding sounds on the wet road. He opened his gaping, black mouth and snorted at her. His eyes — *all of their eyes* — glowed orange-red. *Hellfire.*

Tears streaming and nose running, Jane pedaled like mad. Through blurry eyes, she focused on getting home, and putting distance between herself and the Harker house and Sunshine Falls.

She also looked for signs that anyone was home in the neighbouring houses. Though it was getting late, it wasn't the middle of the night — surely, people would still be awake and puttering around. But not a single light was on anywhere. Even the streetlights hadn't kicked on.

Jane didn't have time to dwell on the eeriness. She had to get home. She wished that her mom would be there, but she had the overnight shift and wouldn't roll in until maybe 5 a.m. That she wouldn't be able to bury herself in her mom's arms made her breathing hitch and her tears burn hotter.

I want my mom.

And then the bike tipped forward. The back tire was in the air, catapulting Jane toward the ground. She cried out, gripping the handlebars. Her legs tried to pedal, but the bike wouldn't move. Something jammed the front wheel.

Bucked off, she hit the pavement. The road scraped her palms and forehead. The bike crashed into her and fell aside. Before she blacked out for a few seconds, she fretted about what her mom was going to say about not wearing a helmet.

She was only out for a few seconds, but it was enough time for the Harker children to catch up. She shook her head, trying to sit up, but something heavy held her leg down. Emma, hugging a charred rabbit, sat on her.

Jane groaned, looking at the bike. A long stick stuck out of the spokes. One of the children had thrown it like a javelin.

Olivia and Noah loomed over her. They swayed in and out of focus as Jane rubbed her head. She wiped away blood, discovering a gash across her forehead.

"Oh…"

As she rolled onto her side, she narrowly avoided the huge stick that Noah jabbed down at her. It cracked against the pavement where she had just been laying. Then Olivia, eyes burning red, cut in.

Jane kicked Emma off. The girl was small, but heavier than she looked. She snapped her teeth at Jane.

Somewhere far away, a house light came on. It was just enough to cast a shine on the children's pale, inhuman faces. But the house was too far away to give Jane any hope. Not as the three monsters dragged her back into the middle of the street. Back toward the house.

She screamed, fighting them. Their little hands held like reinforced steel. She couldn't pry them off.

She squirmed free of her jacket, leaving it in Noah and Emma's grip. The cold night air chilled her bare arms, but she was free — until Olivia clocked her over the back of the head with Noah's big stick.

Jane dropped to her knees before hitting the pavement. Lights out.

When she woke up, she found herself in the clutches of the Beast.

CHAPTER 16

Never in a million years would Barbara Stanley call herself a hero.

She was born in Germany to Canadian parents. Because Dad served in the military, Barbie (and her mom and brother) followed him around the world to different army postings. By the time she was seventeen and her dad had finally been given a permanent position on Canadian soil, Barbie had lived in four different countries and about seven different cities. This migratory lifestyle forced upon her made it difficult to make friends. It also made studying a challenge, and she often struggled to catch up to her peers.

That's not to say she was dumb. In fact, Barbie was very well read, burying her nose in books to find friends, however imaginary. She always managed to catch up on her schoolwork and settle into her new life — just as dad would uproot the family again.

While her older brother, Joey, would put up a fight and rage about having to give up his new sports team or his latest collection of friends, Barbie would quietly retreat to her room and start packing. She would dream about a fresh start and all the ways she would try harder to make friends at the next school. Although, when she started at the next school, she would inevitably stick her foot in her mouth or do something so painfully awkward that the other kids would avoid her.

When they moved to Morganville, Barbie actually looked forward to her first day — because the timing of their move coincided with the first day of school for all the high school students in the district. For once, she could just be the new kid, and not the weird girl starting in May, only to fade into the summer to pop up again in September as a loner. Or disappear completely.

Barbie wasn't a loner; she was lonely.

She soon realized that Morganville High was no different from her other schools, and though she could experiment with a new palette of makeup or try to tame her wild tangle of spirally, auburn curls, she was still what her mean, dead grandma would call "pudgy." Barbie had a round face and a double chin, with a small nose and eyes accentuating how much of a freckled face she had.

Freckles — she despised them more than Joey's obnoxious sports friends. And she hated when the cute boy in her favourite books would meet a cute girl, touch her face, and tell her how amazing and beautiful her freckles were. Barbie wanted to rip the page out and scream at the characters, *No one thinks freckles are cute! They're gross!*

But Barbie would never hurt a book. Books kept her sane, they kept her from falling into a pit of depression. Or from at least realizing she was in the pit.

Her first day of school was a hot mess. She got lost trying to find her classroom after another student gave her terrible directions, and having a bad sense of direction herself, Barbie ended up fifteen minutes late to class. The teacher then berated her in front of her classmates, using her as an example of how to get into his bad graces. Barbie tried to bury her head in the orientation segment of the class and fade into the background, but the teacher kept picking on her. The more the teacher picked, the more the other kids stared.

What's wrong with the new girl?

Barbie's skin burned under their dull-eyed gazes, but she never burst into flames, as much as she prayed for it. As soon as the bell rang, she tried to run for the door, but the teacher blocked her escape.

"Where do you think *you're* going?"

Biting her lip, she peered up at the clock on the wall. "Umm, next class?"

"The bell doesn't dismiss you. *I* dismiss you."

She skulked back to her desk. Just as her butt grazed the hard plastic seat and she squeezed her belly back behind the hardwood desktop, the scowling teacher clapped his hands and dismissed the students.

Barbie made sure she wasn't late to the next class — and that she hid herself at the back of the room.

What she didn't know was that the students from last year had long ago settled on their seating assignments. As she sat there, waiting for the class to start, she heard mutterings about how she may have been sitting in another girl's seat.

"...she's gonna lose it..."

"...maybe a fight...?"

"...cat fight, meow!"

Every muscle in her body felt tensed as she considered finding another spot. She didn't want to sit in the wrong seat, but it looked less and less like she would find another option. So she sat up straight and tried to look like she belonged there.

The bell rang and the class settled. The teacher began to teach — when a mussy-haired girl sauntered in. She didn't have any books with her, just a slim notebook and a pen with its cap bent and chewed. She looked right at Barbie, like, *What the fuck is that blob doing in my spot?* Before she could call Barbie out, the teacher barked at her to sit down.

With no other seats available, the girl had to grab a folding chair from the hallway and share a desk with another student.

Barbie let out a shaky breath.

The girl kept glancing back, glaring at her and then whispering to her desk mate. Barbie felt herself shrinking under this person's wicked energy. So she did what her father jokingly advised about starting at a new school — and what TV sitcoms say about going to prison — and stared the girl down. She put on a scowl far scarier than the first teacher of the morning.

The girl never looked back at her again.

Instead, the girl — who Barbie came to learn was Jane Freeman — led a stealthy campaign to weaken Barbie's confidence (though she had very little to begin with) and made her out to be an obstinate dump truck by gossiping about her to her little friend Lily.

One day, she overheard Jane utter the name that had haunted her these past few months.

The cruel label that sent her home crying when Randy Hukaluk said it to her face during a chemistry lab, even though Randy's last name sounded like a sick cat hocking up a hairball. The nasty nickname quickly replaced her own. Even the cool kids started calling her *The Beast*, as if she were in on the joke.

She just smiled weakly. *Yeah, ha ha. So funny, you guys.* Just another terrible thing to bury deep down inside when she was alone in her room with her books.

But the incident wouldn't stay buried. The memory of Randy's pock-marked face getting up in hers contorted into Jane's snarky face. She slept restlessly that night, and several nights after, plagued by nightmares of being chased and taunted by the jerks at school.

So the next day in art class when she saw Jane, she couldn't take it anymore. She decided to confront her once and for all. But it got out of hand when she clumsily started with, "Leave me alone," bumping into Jane at the same time. Before she could start over, the other kids started chanting. Everyone had it wrong. She didn't want to fight. She just wanted the name-calling and teasing and conspiratorial whispers in the hallways to stop.

But then Jane hurled the paintbrushes, freaking Barbie out so badly that she ran away, and the principal made up his mind, hiding behind a no-tolerance policy for fighting. Barbie got suspended for a week.

Just when it couldn't get any worse, some jerk almost ran her over on her way to a babysitting job, and she had to awkwardly dive out of the way, breaking her ankle when she landed in the gutter.

Fuck my life.

Then, one Saturday night, as she sat in the easy chair by the window of the Fowler house in Sunshine Falls, resting her broken foot after putting the kids to bed, Barbie watched a girl fly off a bike and crash land on her face. It wasn't unusual to see kids do stupid stunts on their bikes and skateboards, but this fall was bad.

Even worse — the girl was Jane and she desperately needed help.

Barbie stalled a bit, hiding behind the curtains and waiting for another neighbour to come to the rescue. But after a while, it was clear that no one else saw what happened. As Barbie peered outside, trying to figure out what to do, three kids ran up to Jane.

Oh, good, she thought. *Someone else can help.*
Because I don't want to.

Does that make me a bad person?

Better than think about it, she returned to her book — interrupted by Jane screaming.

The bloodcurdling sound compelled Barbie to jump up and turn on the porch light. Maybe if the punks outside saw it, they would be scared off and she wouldn't have to worry about her charges, Jaxon and Jayden, waking up and then never going back to sleep.

She opened the door a crack to better hear what was going on.

Jane was laid out on the road, surrounded by the three Harker kids, fairweather friends of the Fowler kids. If there were birthday parties to be had, the Fowlers were there, but Jaxon called them snobby and bossy — especially the older girl, Olivia.

Seemed like a good match for Jane.

Barbie waited for the kids to laugh at Jane as they peeled her off the road. But instead, Noah swung a big stick at her head as Jane rolled aside.

Barbie gasped, covering her mouth. *He almost hit her!*

Olivia had a knife and was about to use it when Jane kicked little Emma. She crawled away as they ripped the jacket off her back and was almost up and on her feet when — *thwack!* — Olivia clobbered her with a small fist.

Jane dropped like a sack of hammers. The children descended.

Barbie didn't think. Hobbling in her medical boot, she threw open the door and limped outside, even though she wasn't one to throw herself into someone else's business.

It was literally her dad's job to jump out of planes and charge into dangerous situations. He said he never blinked — he just did what had to be done. Barbie always thought you had to be a little crazy to be like that.

Maybe she had a touch of what he had.

She screamed and flapped her arms at the children, shooing them away. They stared at the interloper like curious cats. She broke out in goosebumps at the sight of them. *Their eyes... What happened...?*

"Are... are you okay?" she asked, trying to catch her breath.

Noah attacked. She jumped back. He snarled and laughed, reminding her of the kids at school. *See if you can make the big girl jump/cry/scream/jiggle/whatever. See if you can scare the bookworm. What's she gonna do?*

Nothing.

Fear rattled Barbie so deeply to the bone that she couldn't run or cry, so she screeched at them. *"Get away from her!"*

Noah sneered. Then he and Olivia each grabbed one of Jane's ankles, dragging her across the street.

"No!" Barbie shouted. "Stop!"

I have to call the police. But she didn't have a phone. Joey got one when he turned 18, but her parents had a strict rule about cell phones. Something about naked pictures. She glumly didn't want to inform them that nobody was going to ask her for nudes unless they were planning to shame her all over social media. Barbie was no dummy.

But she couldn't let the Harker kids drag Jane off like starving hyenas. So she grabbed Jane under the armpits and yanked her out of their weirdly strong little hands. They stopped dead in their tracks and watched as she half-carried Jane to the Fowler's house, her medical boot scraping along the pavement. Like an injured animal, she couldn't move very fast.

The children trailed behind her. Noah dragged the stick and Olivia rubbed her finger against the knife's blade. Little beads of blood bubbled out. Emma followed, sucking on her thumb. All three of them grinned like maniacs.

Something was definitely wrong with them.

Barbie side-stepped melting snow piles and wet grass, as she hauled the meanest girl in school up the porch and into the house. The Harker kids followed along. They could have overtaken them at any moment. Barbie was slow and Jane was heavier than she looked. The porch steps proved a challenge, and then she couldn't shut the door until Jane's feet crossed the threshold.

She dropped her on the hallway runner so she could turn around and slam the door in their spooky faces. She snapped the lock on just in time — a small hand grabbed the doorknob, twisting it back and forth.

Barbie stumbled backward, nearly stepping on Jane, and wondered, *What is happening?*

CHAPTER 17

Jane groaned as another knock to the back of her head jostled her awake. She tried to see through squinted, sore eyes, but an ornate chandelier over her head was too bright. "What the...?"

Above, little footsteps shuffled closer. *Olivia!*

Jane bolted upright and found herself face to face with the Beast. Before either of them could exchange words, a tiny, sleepy voice asked, "What's that noise?"

Jane looked around, finding herself in a house similar in structure to the Harker house, but with a very different decor style. The furnishings appeared soft and lived in. Nothing white or beige. Big family portraits and photos hung on the walls instead of expensive art. Shoes overflowed off the storage rack by her head, and the house smelled like chili.

"What noise?" asked the Beast, in a surprisingly soft,

quavering voice. "Everything's fine. Go back to bed."

"Why is a girl there?" asked a boy in dump truck pajamas.

"Is she hurt?" asked a second boy in race car pajamas.

"Not quite," said the Beast, unable to look Jane in the eye. "She just has, um, a really bad headache?" Even she didn't believe her own lie.

That made Jane panic. *Why is she lying? What am I doing here? I need to go—*

She scrambled to her feet, the world upending itself like she was a ship in a bottle. The Beast reached out and grabbed her elbow. Jane shook her off and fell toward the door. Holding the doorknob, she peered through the side window and got an eyeful of a maniacal child. The knob turned.

"Don't!" cried the Beast. Jane froze. She didn't know what to do. "I think they're trying to hurt you."

Jane winced, vaguely remembering being hit, but the Beast — *Barbie Stanley*, she heard in Lily's voice — held up her hands and went on.

"I know it sounds weird and you don't have to believe me."

"You *hit* me," Jane said in a small voice, touching her head. There was a tender spot that sent out a wave of pain. She dropped her hand to her side.

"No, I—" Barbie's face burned. She looked down, and then back out the window.

Jane shook her head. *Rather take my chances with the brats—* She went to open the door, peering out at Noah.

He punched his fist against the glass. She jumped back, hands off. Now she wasn't so sure.

His little fist left a bloody print, but it wasn't his hand. He had smashed the delicate body of a small bird against the glass. The tiny, broken corpse flopped to the ground, hitting his shoe on the way down and bouncing into the garden.

Jane spun around. She was done with kids — forever. If her mother had any dream of having grandchildren, she could bury it tomorrow. Jane was done.

"Where are you going?" Barbie asked.

"Back door."

"Wait!" Barbie followed her.

Jane quickened her pace to get the hell out of there and away from the Beast. She needed a head start on the Harkers. As she cut through the kitchen, she banged her hip on the island counter.

Before she made it to the door, two grinning faces peered in through the French doors.

"Shit," Jane muttered.

"You shouldn't go out there." Barbie came up from behind, her belly bumping into her.

Jane spun around, ready to fight. "Get away from me!"

Barbie wobbled backwards, hands up. "Sorry! I—"

"Call 911!"

"Okay, okay, sorry, okay." She shuffled around the counter to the wall phone and dialed 911, shyly looking back at Jane as she spoke to the operator. When she was done giving the address and explaining what was going on, she hung up. "They said there's a higher-than-average number of calls and they'll send a car as soon as possible."

"That's *it?*"

"And we're supposed to stay in the house."

Jane didn't have any intention of hanging around. She wanted to *go home*. She wanted her mom. She wanted to wash off the blood, take an aspirin, and fall into bed. But before she could make any plans or dream any dreams, her knees weakened, and she grabbed onto the counter for support.

Hesitating slightly, Barbie asked, "You okay?"

Jane snapped, "Fuck, no, I'm not okay." She held up her bleeding hand and pointed to the gash on her head. "Those assholes are trying to kill me. They already killed Nate."

"Oh, geez."

Jane stared at Emma and Olivia, lurking outside. "They killed him right in front of me."

"Oh, my god," Barbie whispered, covering her mouth.

"Yeah," said Jane, gingerly picking at her bandage. "Fucking dead."

* * *

Sitting at the bottom of the staircase, Jane and Barbie waited and watched the door. Barbie had to shoo the Fowler boys back to bed before calling their parents' voicemails to beg them to please come home.

Every now and then, one of the Harker children peered

inside at them or tapped on the window, like they were in a fishbowl. Then Olivia asked them to come out and play.

"We won't hurt you," she said, grinning like a big, fat liar.

It wasn't long before a car pulled up out front. "It's RCMP!" Barbie scrambled to look outside. With a sigh, she added, "It's over."

Staying low, Jane crept to the window. The officer was alone. As he got out of the car, he adjusted the cap on his head and surveyed the scene: three children hanging around outside in the cold night with no shoes on. Did he see the knife?

The porchlight blinked off.

"Did you—?" Jane reached around Barbie to turn it back on.

"No," said Barbie, stepping back to show her. The light, for all intents and purposes, was still in the ON position.

"Hey, kids," said the officer. "What're you doing? You live here? Where are your parents?"

They didn't say anything, just formed a line across the porch, each one holding something behind their backs: a knife, a big stick, and a bunny. The hairs on Jane's arms began to rise.

"It's okay," the officer said. "My name is Constable Haggerty and I just want to know what's going on." The children were silent. Haggerty's brows stitched together. He had the hard-lined face of a man who got the shit calls — domestic abuse, car crashes, and god knew what else.

But this was probably the weirdest call of his life. "Someone from this address called 911. I need to know if it was any of you. It's okay if you made a mistake…"

Barbie grabbed the doorknob, but Jane stopped her. "What're you doing?"

"We called," she said. "We have to tell him or he's going to leave."

As Barbie switched off the lock and twisted the knob, Noah spun around and pressed his head against the glass. He glared at her. His breath fogged up the window in front of his face, and for a brief second the two babysitters saw something less than human.

"Don't!" yelped Jane, locking the door. "They're going to kill us."

Barbie's eyes filled with tears, but she didn't resist, and Jane vaguely wondered where the monstrous, bullying girl from school had gone. Because this chick was a wuss.

"Hey." Haggerty's voice boomed, drawing Noah away from the window. "Enough with the silent treatment. What's the deal here? If you don't tell me, I'm calling in your parents."

Yes, fucking please, Jane thought.

After a tense second, Haggerty reached for his shoulder mic. Before he could radio the dispatcher, Olivia stepped down from the porch. She tipped her head down, looking sadly at her socked feet. "We don't live here."

He let go of the mic and pointed to the house. "Have you been bothering the folks inside?"

"We just wanna play," Noah said.

"Well, it's a little late for that, son," he said. "Now move aside. I need to check on the residents."

"They're not very fun," pouted Emma.

When they didn't step aside, Haggerty huffed and marched around them. He stood at the door and it took all of Jane's willpower not to open it and throw herself at him, crying for her mom. But as he raised his fist to knock, Barbie threw open the door instead.

"You're not very fun either," Olivia declared, plunging a knife into the constable's back.

He twisted around, which only added to the damage she had inflicted. The blade speared through his spinal cord, severing his legs from the rest of his body. He dropped to the ground. Olivia sliced him up on his way down.

Tears sprang out of Jane's eyes, blurring her view. The three children surrounded Haggerty and—

Jane shoved Barbie out of the way and slammed the door. Blood splashed across the lower half of the window. Outside, Haggerty groaned and then fell silent.

Barbie started crying and biting her knuckles.

Shivering, Jane collapsed on the stairs and held her head in her bloody hands.

CHAPTER 18

The babysitters weren't coming out and that made the children very angry. *Come out, come out, wherever you are* — that was the law of the playground. If you were going to play games, you had to follow the rules.

Like never giving up on a friend or never breaking a promise. The Harker children wouldn't let Zed down, and with his influence and strength, he wouldn't let them down either.

Nor would he let them go.

Not yet. Not until they finished the game.

Kill the babysitter.

After the police officer collapsed on the porch, the children tore into him. Their small fingers grew sharp and deadly. Elongated fingernails pierced his belly, ripping open his flesh and tearing out his guts. No one saw or heard a thing. Except for the babysitters.

Anyone passing on the street would have seen them. In such a new neighbourhood, there was hardly any foliage or greenery to conceal a murder. But no one was out tonight. Something in the air — negative energy, an impending late winter storm, a drop in temperature — kept the residents of Sunshine Falls behind their locked doors and curled up safe under their blankets.

The children needed reinforcements, so they joined hands and put out a call. An invitation.

The more the merrier.

Anyone on the block might have felt an infrasound-like sensation rumbling beneath the surface of their boring lives. A migraine or a series of disturbing dreams. The adults were lucky — Zed couldn't reach them.

Not yet.

But twenty children on the block heard the call. They sat up suddenly as if an invisible puppeteer jerked on their strings and called them to attention. They were mostly barefooted and clad in rocket ship/dinosaur/Hello Kitty/Wonder Woman pajamas, an army of little people. They climbed out of their beds, wandering across toy-strewn carpets, silently leaving their cozy houses for the dark street.

Along the way, they grabbed knives, scissors, box cutters, and knitting needles.

Their parents never noticed a thing.

* * *

Barbie kept dialing 911. Each time, a recorded voice told her to stay on the line. She nodded, as if the mechanical voice could see her, and then winced painfully when the call disconnected. She was about to call for a fourth time, when Jane hung up for her.

"What?" Barbie whined.

Jane shook her head. "No one's coming."

"Someone has to come." Her voice was shrill. "There's a-a-a... a *dead police officer outside!*"

Jane shushed her. *"I know!* But you freaking out isn't gonna change anything." She pointed up. "And if your kids come down here, they're gonna freak the fuck out."

Barbie's face scrunched up and she bit down on her knuckles. "I hate this."

"Me too."

The two teens looked at each other. Bully and victim under one roof, talking civilly to each other. It was pretty fucking weird. For the first time in forever, Jane forgot she was on Barbie's shit list, and being around Barbie for this long made her wonder why she ever thought the girl was scary.

Jane took a jar of pickles out of the fridge. When she couldn't open it because of her injured hand, she meekly held it out to Barbie. "Little help?"

"How can you eat at a time like this?" But Barbie opened it for her with one good twist. She handed it back with the lid still on so the brine water wouldn't slosh all over the floor. Jane set the lid on the counter and scooped out a pickle.

"It's been a hell of a night."

"So what're we going to do?" Barbie asked.

"The hell if I know," she replied. "They've been awful quiet out there." *Too quiet.*

"No one's going to save us unless they think something's wrong," said Barbie. "The kids are too quiet, and the only thing people in Sunshine worry about is teenagers throwing loud parties." She rubbed her chin. "So ... if we had a big party with lots of noise, someone else would call the cops or maybe come over to yell at us."

"And then we might be saved," Jane finished.

They smiled, but then Barbie shook her head. "We can't. You just said Jaxon and Jayden could come down here. I don't want to scare them."

"Who?"

"The kids I'm babysitting."

"Oh, right. Well, special circumstances." Jane threw open cupboards and dragged out every pot and pan she could find. "Tell them to cover their ears. Hell, call them down to help! Kids are really good at being annoying." She put a large saucepan on her head like she was going to war and asked, "Where's the stereo?"

* * *

After showing Jane where to find the Fowler's built-in home audio system, Barbie slipped away to check on the kids. She was worried about them; worried that the noise would frighten them, or that they would somehow see Constable Hagerty's body on the porch.

I'll just tell them to stay in their room. No matter what. Just stay inside and wait for me to come get them.

She limped upstairs, each step creaking under her weight. The medical boot tapping with each step. She held onto the rail for balance, flinching when Jane began to blast heavy metal. It sounded like Ozzy or Iron Maiden or any of those artists her dad like listening to on the classic rock station. To Barbie, it all sounded like a helicopter caught in a tin can, but it was loud, proud, and rattling the walls.

The Fowlers had a three-bedroom house of which the boys shared a room. Barbie couldn't imagine having to share a room with her brother.

As she got to the door, cold air blew across her feet. Something was wrong on the other side.

She slowly turned the knob. The bright light of the moon filled the room. Specks of snow floated in through the open window, where the screen had been shredded, leaving a gap big enough for a small child or two to sneak through.

Barbie almost screamed. She covered her mouth with her hand, tucking her knuckles between her chattering teeth and biting down.

Rumpled sheets and comforters thrown aside; the beds were empty. The children were gone.

CHAPTER 19

The music was turned up so loud, Jane felt the vibrations through the floor — and yet, it didn't drown out Barbie's anguished sob.

She looked up as Barbie leaned over the railing. Her face was flushed, cheeks puffing in and out. She opened her mouth to say something and instead began to cry, slumping down on the floor.

Jane's heart stopped. She ran upstairs, not wanting to be left alone. She took thestairs two at a time and tumbled down next to Barbie, outside the children's bedroom. "What's wrong?"

"They're gone."

"Who?"

Barbie blubbered and pointed to the room.

The Fowler children.

More goddamn children.

She went to see for herself — maybe they were hiding.

She felt weird standing in someone else's room. She couldn't even stand to be in her mom's room, and she was perfectly welcome there. Nights when she was struck down with a fever, she would crawl into her bed — if her mom wasn't working some ridiculous night shift. Her mom would give her sips of icy water and stroke her hair, and they would watch infomercials on her small TV.

It definitely looked like boys lived here. Toys scattered all about, clothes balled up and left in random corners, and their beds were unmade. *No, they're not in bed, that's the problem.* The window was wide open and the screen had a big tear in it.

Jane went to the window. Drawing a deep breath, she braced herself for the image of two small broken bodies on the ground below.

But no bodies. Nobody at all. Just a big tree branch that scraped against the siding. If they were bold enough, the kids could have climbed onto the branch and descended the tree.

She backed out of the room and returned to Barbie. "They're gone."

"I know!" cried Barbie. *"I'm not stupid!"*

"Where would they go?"

"I don't know! Your evil kids probably hurt them, probably lured them outside and—" The thought was too horrible to finish.

"They're not *my* kids! I'm just the babysitter!"

"You're supposed to watch them! You're supposed to

take care of them. How did you let this happen?"

A light went on in her brain. More of an alert — a reminder that Barbie was still a bitch. Jane berated herself for letting her guard down. She looked down at her feet. "I don't know."

Barbie sniffed as she got to her feet and headed downstairs.

"Where are you going?" asked Jane.

At the door, Barbie pulled on her regular boot and put on her coat. "I have to find them."

"Why?"

She glared. "What do you mean *why?* I can't leave them out there! It's freezing and they're in their pajamas! And your kids just *killed* somebody!"

"Never took you for a responsible babysitter type," Jane muttered, crossing her arms.

Barbie frowned. "What does that mean? Why would you say that? You think I'm not a good babysitter?"

Jane couldn't think of a better response than, *Because I'm not a good sitter. I'm just in it for the money. Cold, hard cash. I'm an irresponsible monster. Maybe I'm the real beast. Because Barbie's kids are missing and mine are demonic cop killers.*

Barbie wiped away fresh tears and threw one last dirty look at Jane before opening the door.

"Wait!" Jane called, running after her.

The police car faced the house, its engine revving. High beams blinded them. Someone sat behind the wheel. Someone who could barely reach the pedals.

Eyes adjusting to the brightness, Jane and Barbie cowered together at the threshold.

Children. So many children. From greasy-faced pre-teens to thumb-sucking toddlers, children had gathered on the lawn. Some lingered in the street. All stared at the house, mouths curled into rotten grins. Neither babysitter could see their eyes, but had they been able to, they would have seen embers burning in their pupils — frightening, but not quite the same hellfire that consumed the eyes of Olivia, Noah, and Emma.

"Play with us, Jane," hissed one young voice.

Jane hooked an arm around Barbie and pulled her inside. She didn't have to put in too much effort. Barbie was eager to get away. Jane slammed and locked the door, leaning against it.

"What the hell is going on?"

"I saw them," said Barbie. "Jaxon and Jayden are out there."

"Yeah, and so is every kid on the block."

"What's happening?"

"I have no fucking clue."

"But how did we get here? What happened tonight?"

"I don't know!" Jane cried.

This time Barbie grabbed her and gave her a shake. Tears sprang out of her eyes. Was the Beast finally going to get her revenge? Throw Jane to the wolves and watch the children tear her apart?

"You can't freak out now," Barbie said. "Tell me everything that happened tonight. Maybe there's a way we can backtrack to some important detail."

"I don't know…" *I don't want to do this anymore. I don't want to think about it.*

Barbie persisted. "Maybe there's a way we can fix this. There has to be something we can do."

Trembling all over, Jane shook her head. She braced herself for Barbie to slap some sense into her, but the girl pulled her into a bear hug and patted her back. Rigid and surprised, Jane carefully set her head on the girl's shoulder.

"It's okay," said Barbie. "We'll figure this out. We'll save them."

As much as Jane hated other people touching — or god forbid, *hugging* — her, she nodded, even though she didn't care about saving anybody but herself.

Finally, Barbie let go and gently squeezed Jane's shoulder. "It's going to be okay. We'll come up with a plan… Figure something out."

"We were playing games," she said.

"Huh?"

"We were playing with a Ouija board before this all happened," Jane explained. "We'd been playing with it for a while."

"How long?"

Jane shrugged. "I don't know… A couple of weeks, maybe?"

"A couple of *weeks?*"

"They showed me something … insane. Like, when we played with this spirit, he would grant wishes."

"Like a genie? That's two separate things."

"I know, but it really worked. They wished for their parents to get *divorced* — how sick is that?"

"Very sick," she agreed. "What did you wish for?"

"Uh..."

"Well, wouldn't you? Isn't that why you'd play with it so much?"

Barbie read her like an open book. Jane felt her cheeks burn, thinking about all the things she wished for. One in particular.

I wish something bad would happen to the Beast.

"It was just supposed be a stupid game," she said. "This ... spirit or whatever just liked to play games and shit, and if you played along, he'd grant wishes. And the kids were nuts about it. I didn't mean for anything bad to happen.

Except for when I did.

"Then maybe we have to go back and make another wish," said Barbie. "Wish for all of this to stop and go back to normal."

Jane wasn't sure if it would be that easy.

Outside, police sirens whooped. Red and blue lights swirled around, bouncing off the walls inside the Fowler house. The babysitters pressed their faces to the window, hoping that the cavalry had arrived.

There was only one police car parked out front — Constable Haggerty's. It flashed its lights and revved its engine one final time before blasting off from the curb and heading straight for them.

Jane screamed and grabbed Barbie, shoving her toward the stairs. They ran up, up, up, crawling over each other to the second floor as the car drove up the porch and smashed into the front door. The airbags exploded in the child driver's face, knocking him out.

Jane didn't bother to look back to see who it was. It didn't matter. All the kids on the block wanted her dead now, and with the door busted open, they swarmed inside, searching for bodies.

Luckily for the sitters, the possessed children didn't notice that Jane and Barbie had fled upstairs to hide in Jaxon and Jayden's bedroom.

With no lock on the boys' bedroom door and no time to find another hiding spot, Jane and Barbie had to make do. They couldn't even move any furniture to barricade the door without alerting the children to their location.

Please, please, please think we escaped out the back door, Jane prayed.

But the back door was locked. If she had learned anything as a babysitter, it was that children were not as stupid as she wanted to believe. And possessed children were even smarter.

They're gonna find us.

Barbie's chest heaved as she tried to keep calm. Jane pulled her into the cramped, cluttered closet, kicking aside piles of dirty clothes and soiled socks to make room. Then she eased Barbie down in one corner and closed the doors.

"What now?" Barbie whispered.

I wish I knew, thought Jane, biting her tongue.

CHAPTER 20

The children drifted through the house like wispy clouds across a full moon. They were silent, searching everywhere: the basement, upstairs, backyard.

Olivia stood at the bottom of the stairs. One hand gripped the railing, nails digging into the wood. One foot on the second step, ready to bound upward at the first sign of the babysitters. She had no ill will against either of them because this was all in good fun. Catch a babysitter by her toe. And if the other girl got swept up in the chaos, well... that was just the name of the game.

Collateral damage — she didn't know what that meant, but the words flowed through her mind.

Kill the babysitter.

She would do whatever was needed to win, even if that meant letting her brother get behind the wheel of a police car and crash it into a house. It was a stupid idea, but also brilliant. The teenagers weren't going to let them in — not by the hairs on their chinny-chin-chins — but the trade-off was that Noah had been punched in the face by an airbag. He laid unconscious behind the wheel as the other children tore the house apart.

Leave him.

While she didn't know where Jane could have gotten to, she knew she was inside the house. *Come out, come out wherever you are...* Glaring into the darkness upstairs, she knew Jane was hiding.

The straw-haired morons she once knew as Jaxon and Jayden drifted through the master bedroom and down the hall to the two remaining bedrooms and bathroom.

Through Olivia, Zed seethed. *Find them. Find those bitches.*

* * *

"We're gonna die, aren't we?" Barbie whispered. She covered her mouth with her hands, as if that would block out the sound to anyone else but Jane.

Jane shushed her.

"I don't hear anything."

"Just calm down," Jane hissed.

Barbie wriggled between two shelves of a poorly constructed closet system. Her big shoulders were wedged in. She felt stuck and tried to think of the awful missions her dad had been on. He was a big guy and he had been through worse than this. She wondered what he would do now.

I bet he'd find a way to get back to that Ouija board and end this. She gave Jane a shrewd look. *He wouldn't be selfish.*

But her dad was made of different stuff than most people. Jane Freeman, on the other hand, was like most people Barbie had encountered. Cold, mean bullies who didn't care about anyone but themselves.

I'll have to do it myself, she thought, trembling.

They watched and waited. The bedroom door opened. Two boys slipped inside like shadows. They walked to the open window and stuck their heads out. Without saying a word, they clamored back out of the room.

Barbie covered her mouth, not trusting herself not to make a sound. *They think we went out the window!*

Neither babysitter said anything until the boys closed the door behind them and ran down the stairs. A few more doors slammed and then the house was still.

Jane slumped against a pile of shirts and pants. "Shit," she grunted. "Finally."

"Are you sure?" asked Barbie. "It could be a trick."

Jane gave her a tired, humorless grin. "The dumb kids think we climbed out the window. Now they're gonna go running through the neighbourhood looking for us. We're home free."

"We have to fix this."

"Fix what?" Jane asked.

"I thought you were just mean," Barbie said, shaking

her head, "but are you stupid too?"

Jane flinched.

Barbie feared she went too far, but she didn't let up. "You're not gonna do anything about the Ouija board, are you? What if someone else gets hurt?"

Jane moped. "I just want to go home."

Barbie plucked something that looked like lint off the boys' floor. "I guess you really *don't* care about anyone else," she moped.

"Excuse me?" Jane puffed out her chest. "You don't know anything about me."

"I know you're a m-mean bitch."

Barbie covered her mouth. She couldn't believe those words escaped her. And she couldn't run away. She was trapped in a closet with her worst nightmare — and then she called her a bitch.

"What the fuck?" said Jane, her voice louder than it should have been. "You've been making my life a living hell since you moved here."

* * *

I'm a mean bitch? No way.

"I've never bullied you," Jane said.

"You and your popular friends call me a beast and you laugh at me behind my back," said Barbie, cheeks red. Wedged pathetically between two shelves, she couldn't even look at Jane, but Jane saw a silver tear roll down her face. "I didn't want anything except to be left alone."

"You've been making *my* life a living hell."

"How?" Barbie cried.

Jane couldn't think of a solid answer, other than that she had been living in fear. But was it possible she had built up that fear all on her own? An overactive imagination can be a dangerous thing.

"I'm not a bully," said Jane, defensively. "You're the one who attacked me in art class."

"But only because—" Barbie stopped herself and looked at the closet door slats.

"Only because *what?"* Jane hissed.

Barbie's lips twitched and her throat spasmed as she choked on her own words. It went on like that for a while, and then: "The Beast thing started with you."

Jane's stomach turned. "No, it didn't." But didn't it? She wasn't so sure of the name's origin. "It was just a joke."

"Well, it wasn't funny to me."

"How did you—"

"Oh, you mean how did I find out about the worst kept secret at school? When all the guys come up to me and call me Beast? How could I *not* know?"

"It was just an inside joke, just between me and—"

"Lily. Yeah, I know. I asked her in the bathroom one day and she spilled her guts. Said you started it."

"Lily..." She groaned, rolling her head against the wall.

"I think she thought I was going to beat her up," said Barbie. "She also told me that you bully her too. You bully everyone. You're mean to anyone who isn't popular. And you act like you're so cool, but no one likes you either."

Jane tried to swallow, but it felt like nails in her throat.

"And thanks to you I've got this ... stupid reputation." She shook her head as if she could shake away her tears. "I'm not a bad person. I want to be pretty and have friends too. It sucks being ignored and forgotten about, but you know what's worse? When everyone around you thinks you're a beast."

CHAPTER 21

What a bitch, was Jane's first thought after Barbie's embarrassing confession. She would have stormed out if they were in any other situation. Hell, in any other situation, she wouldn't be stuck in a closet with the scariest girl in school. Trapped, however, she clenched her jaw and listened to Barbie weep silently and breathlessly into her hands.

I'm the bully. She didn't believe it. Everyone was the hero in their own story. Barbie could believe whatever she wanted if that made her feel better about the monster she had become. But *was* she really a monster? After spending this much time with her, Jane began to doubt everything she had ever thought about the girl. And that was dangerous because what if it was all a trick?

Jane had always considered herself one of the downtrodden unpopular kids. People avoided her like the plague. Teachers seemed sick of her and the only guy that had ever shown any interest didn't know her very well because he was new in town.

And now he's dead.

And Lily, her best friend, her *only* friend, was afraid of her.

Jane's whole world began to crumble. *I have to get out of here.* She reached for the closet door.

"What are—?" Barbie tried to stand up, bumping into Jane, as the closet doors flew open. The two babysitters froze.

Olivia found them.

Jane jumped back as the girl reached in, but Barbie didn't move as quickly. Olivia dragged her out.

Jane launched after them. *"Get off!"* She tackled Olivia. Her elbow hit the floor. Pain exploded throughout her arm. She bit down on her tongue and squeezed her eyes shut. When she opened them, Olivia stood on the nightstand between the two beds.

Barbie tried to pull Jane back into the closet, but it was too late to hide.

Holding up her knife, Olivia opened her mouth to scream.

Jane leaped up and with one punch, hit the girl. Olivia wobbled on the nightstand. The lamp tumbled onto one of the beds; Olivia fell toward the window. She tried grabbing the frame to stop herself, but the girl slipped through the screen and disappeared.

Barbie gasped.

Jane stared at the empty space where Olivia had just been.

"Oh, fuck. Oh, no."

Barbie ran to the window and looked down. She let out an anguished cry and turned to Jane. "She's…"

Jane already knew what she was going to say. *I killed someone… I killed a little girl…*

<Bad babysitter.>

Many pairs of small feet stomped up the stairs.

Jane tumbled down a guilt spiral, unable to make sense of the racket coming their way.

<Bad babysitter.>
<Bad babysitter.>
<Bad babysitter.>

—was all she could hear until Barbie yelled at her to grab the dresser. Moving robotically, she did as she was told. They dragged the boys' dresser to the door to keep the children out.

On the other side of the door, the children pounded and punched to get in.

"This isn't going to hold," said Barbie. "We have to get out of here."

Jane nodded distantly.

<Bad babysitter.>

"We have to get the Ouija board and take all of this back," she said. "Maybe wish it all away."

Jane began to get the shakes and Barbie grabbed her shoulders.

"Don't lose it on me," she said. "We have to do this."

"What if it doesn't work?"

Barbie gulped. "We have to try."

* * *

Barbie led the way, surprising Jane with how quickly and stealthily she stepped out onto the tree branch and scaled down the rough trunk. Barbie was halfway down when she looked back up at Jane, watching her from the window.

"Come on!"

With her first step, Jane missed the branch. The wind was blowing so hard, whipping her hair around her face, she almost couldn't see. She fell forward, arms pinwheeling. When she smacked against the trunk, she held onto it for dear life.

"Hurry!" Barbie cried. She had made it to the bottom, broken ankle and all.

Jane couldn't look down, nor could she let go of the tree. *What if I fall? What if I land on top of Olivia? What is Mrs. Harker going to think about—?*

And even if she made it down, she was going to have to go back to the Harkers' house. She would have to walk past Nate's body.

And she would be back where she started and farther from home.

She gripped the tree. "I can't do it."

"You're almost there," Barbie lied.

"I-I can't."

"You have to. We're losing our head start."

Jane shook her head and hugged the tree even harder.

"No, seriously — you have to get down. The branch is broken."

Jane looked down at the branch under her foot. She hadn't noticed the big crack, though it did feel unstable under her weight. But she had never climbed a tree before, and didn't all trees feel so ... loose?

The branch snapped. She shrieked, riding down the side of the tree, breaking through weak, brittle branches until a big one near the bottom just about split her in two. She tilted sideways, letting go, reaching for the earth. Her wrist bend under, sending a sharp spasm through her arm.

Barbie helped her up. "Ooh, that looked bad. Are you okay?"

Jane clutched it to her chest. "I don't know. Let's just get out of here."

"Are we doing this?" Barbie asked solemnly.

"Are you asking me if I'm gonna chicken out?" *Yes, I would totally chicken out. If a cop or my mom were to miraculously come by to save me, I will run for the fucking hills. I will never step foot in the Harker house again. But right now, I have no choice.* Jane took a deep breath. "I wanna get this over with."

"I'm coming with you," Barbie said.

Jane felt her knees weaken at the thought. Someone else to carry this burden and do this bizarre task? *Yes, please.* "No, this is my fault ... probably. Why don't you find the cops or something?"

Barbie rubbed her arms, fighting against the cold. "Come on — a bunch of little kids drove a car into a house. It was the loudest thing I've ever heard, and *not one* neighbor came out to see what's going on? No one peeked out a window and called the police? Something's *seriously* wrong here."

"Huh," said Jane. "I didn't even notice…"

"Yeah, well, I had to think about something while I was waiting for you to fall to your—"

Death.

They paused at the feet-end of Olivia, staring blankly up at the sky. Jane nudged her small foot.

The dead girl sprang up into a seated position. She growled, picked up the knife that had fallen next to her and stabbed at Jane.

Jane stumbled backwards, bumping into Barbie, and the two babysitters broke into a run.

CHAPTER 22

As the babysitters dashed out of the yard and onto the street, the children were hot on their tails. Olivia blended into the mob and sprinted to the front. She pumped her tiny arms, knife still in hand, hungry for blood.

Kill the babysitter!

Jane wheezed for air, clutching at Barbie's elbow. She was surprised at how fast the other girl could move, even with the clunky medical boot turning her gait into a limp. "I can't ... run ... any ... longer."

"Don't stop!" Barbie barked. She sounded like a drill sergeant. "Keep moving! Come on!"

The house wasn't far, just across the street, but the children were fast — and gaining on them. *Do they know where we're going?* Jane wondered as her foot splashed down in an icy puddle. *Fuck!*

Almost there. The babysitters stormed up the steps to the Harker house. The door was closed, and Jane feared it would be locked. *We can't get in. We're trapped. They'll swarm us, rip our guts out. I don't wanna die. I don't wanna—*

She grabbed the handle, pressed the lock down, and they barreled into the foyer. Jane stopped suddenly and Barbie slammed into her. They spun around, shutting the door in Olivia's enraged face. The girl howled as Barbie locked her out.

Jane bent over, catching her breath. Bile lurched up to her throat and she bolted upright to keep her guts down. Her lungs burned badly from the sprint; she didn't need to add to the pain by puking.

"Where's the board?" Barbie asked.

Jane pointed in the general direction of the kitchen. "That way... Basement..."

"Okay," she said, heading in that direction. "Let's go."

"Hold up," said Jane. "This isn't about you."

"It's about me now," replied Barbie.

"No, I put you through enough." *Even before tonight.* "Just wait here and tell me if any of those brats is about to turn this place into another drive-thru."

"You can't do it alone."

It seemed crazy to believe that a Ouija board could cause this much trouble, but Barbie was right. She couldn't do this alone.

She led Barbie through the kitchen and paused at the basement door, looking down the stairs.

"Okay, so... Nate's down there... It's not good."

Barbie nodded, eyes watering. "Okay."

"Wait." She dashed around to the knife block and drew out two steak knives. She handed one to Barbie. "Just in case those kids get too close."

Barbie took it with a shaking hand. "I don't know if I can use this."

"It's a knife," said Jane. "It's easy."

"I don't want to hurt anybody."

Jane let out a shaky breath. Relieved that she hadn't killed Olivia, some of her old bravado had returned — even though she hoped she never had to use the knives. "Well, we'll have to do what we have to do."

Barbie swallowed. "My dad's in the army, but I don't know if he's ever killed anybody."

"He probably has," said Jane, as they descended the staircase. "You never asked him?"

"Feels weird. I know my brother bugs him about it. He says no, but I don't know. I feel like I would lie to my kids about that."

"Then he probably has," said Jane.

The basement was dark. Made darker when Jane shut the door behind them. The kids had turned out the lights before they chased her out of the house. *Or a demonic presence has escaped out of the Ouija board and is now suffocating all the light*, thought Jane. The basement felt colder than outside. She sniffled, nose aching and running from the chill.

"It's so cold..." said Barbie.

Jane fumbled along the wall until she found the light switch. She flicked it on. The carpet where the fire broke out was still a soggy, black mess. Nate's body lay sprawled face down on the floor. Almost forgotten.

A lump thickened in Jane's throat. *I left him alone in a strange house.* She glanced at Barbie who cupped her mouth. Her wide, teary eyes stared at the body. Jane blocked her view, pulling her away.

"Don't look," she said.

"Too late," Barbie whispered. "Wh-what happened?"

"They... they cut his throat," she said.

"At least he looks ... peaceful."

As they rounded up the Ouija board and planchette, Jane glanced back at him. He did look peaceful, but only because all his muscles relaxed when he died.

"Okay, so how do we end this?" Jane asked, setting the planchette in the middle of the board. Like a key in a lock — time to open the door.

Barbie knelt down with her. "I don't know exactly."

"I thought you were the expert."

"I've only read a few books and played it a couple of times with my cousins. That doesn't make me an expert. You're the one who was making wishes on it. How were you doing that?"

"I told you — I don't know!"

Bang! The front door burst open. The children ran inside, their feet pounding on the floor above. Jane and Barbie exchanged a look. If the possessed children had managed to break through the heavy front door, they would make quick work of the flimsy interior one.

Instead of twenty pairs of feet racing around, the children stopped at the basement door. Occasionally the floorboards creaked and groaned, but otherwise the kids seemed in no hurry to barge in.

I don't like this, Jane thought.

Barbie snapped her fingers, bringing her attention back to the board. "Come on. What do we do?"

Jane shrugged. "Just talk to it?"

"I don't want to talk to it," said Barbie. "This is your problem, remember? *You* need to do this."

"Fine, okay." Jane frowned and focused on the board. "Hello? Is Zed there?" She looked at Barbie as the planchette slowly glided around. "Are you moving it?"

"I think we're both moving it," she replied.

HELLO.

"Shit." Jane wanted to leap back.

"Do it," Barbie said.

"Uh, hi," she said. "Uh, I wish to make everything go back to normal."

Jane almost couldn't follow along with the letters as the planchette pointed them out.

THAT'S NOT HOW THIS WORKS.

"How then?"

PLAY THE GAME.

"What game?"

KILL THE BABYSITTER

"I don't want to play anymore," she said, glimpsing Barbie's pale, frightened face. "I never wanted to play. I wish to end this game."

NO.

I GRANT THE WISHES.

YOU PLAY THE GAME.

"Fuck you, we're done."

"Jane..." warned Barbie.

"No, this is bullshit," she said, sweeping the planchette to the bottom of the board. "If you won't help us, I'm done. *Goodbye."*

The planchette suddenly weighed a hundred pounds. It wouldn't budge, like it had embedded itself in the board. And then it only moved of its own volition.

NO.

"Um, yes," replied Jane. "Goodbye. Go away. *The end.* Control-alt-delete. Transmission *over."* She stared at Barbie. "What if he won't go away?"

"I don't know."

Whatever Zed was, he was strong — and powerful enough to control children from afar.

Jane trembled. As she took a deep breath to calm herself, she smelled smoke. "Do you smell that?"

YES.

"It's smoke!" Barbie pointed to the basement door. Jane craned her neck to see dark plumes of smoke billowed down from upstairs.

"They're trying to smoke us out!"

Hands slipping off the planchette, Barbie got ready to cut and run, but Jane grabbed her. "Wait, don't leave!"

Tears watered Barbie's eyes. *"I don't wanna die."*

"We're not gonna die. *Please*. We just have to make this thing say goodbye."

"I have to go. My mom and dad—"

"We'll break a window!" cried Jane.

Barbie's face crinkled as she looked at the narrow windows. "I won't fit."

"Fuck," Jane sighed. She wanted to scream but forced herself to choke it down. There was enough panic in the air already. "Okay, let's…" She forced Barbie's hand back down on the planchette and asked Zed, "We'll play, okay? *Okay?* What do we have to do?"

Shaking her head and crying, Barbie tried to pull away. "I don't want to. I want to go home. This was a bad idea."

"It was *your* idea." She held Barbie's hand. "Don't leave me."

Barbie wept. "O-okay. What do we do?"

The planchette began to move again, interrupting the girls. They watched it with wide, watering eyes as the smoke filled the room.

LET'S PLAY.

CHAPTER 23

Feeling lightheaded from the smoke, Jane awaited Zed's instructions. She imagined the police finding their corpses in the morning and having to tell her mother what a dumbass she was.

Mrs. Freeman, your daughter was probably on drugs. What idiot would keep playing a board game while a fire rages above? Seems like she deserved to die. Natural selection, am I right?

Jane snapped. *"What are you waiting for?"*

By now, smoke filled the basement. It stung her eyes, and she tried wiping her face on her arm. When she blinked them, she could barely see Barbie sitting right in front of her. *We're so dead. It's too late.*

Behind Barbie, who sniffled and stared at the board, a cloudy figure swayed. Something that shouldn't have been there. Like a shadow without a person, weaving in and out of the smoke.

I'm losing it, she thought. There was no way anyone else had gotten in. She was delusional. *This is the end.*

"Jane...?" Barbie leaned toward her. "Are you okay?"

Jane felt herself slipping away, disappearing in time. Her eyes burned, yet she could see it — a man's shape forming out of the smoke. And yet not a man. He had the same jerky movements of the possessed children.

Barbie was far, far away now. Her voice distant and fading fast.

<Jane, hello,> said the man.

"Who ... are you?"

<I'm Zed.>

Her arms moved. She held the planchette, still engaged with the Ouija board, but now a new player had entered the game. *"This isn't a game."*

<Of course it's a game.>

"I don't wanna play anymore."

<Then you'll lose.>

"I don't care. Just make the kids normal again. Take my car and my phone..."

<I already have. And I still want to play.>

"Well, I don't."

<No one does. Because you're all no fun at the end. Did you know that even suicidal people change their minds at the last second? It's usually too late and they die a screaming, horrible death. Fun fact!>

Jane felt nauseous. *"Goodbye."*

<We're not done yet.> The planchette held firm.

She looked down and saw a dark smoky hand covering hers. *"Please."*

<*You're no fun anymore. I don't want to play with you.*>

"Fine. Let me go back to the way things were."

<*Only if you finish the game.*>

"Whatever. What do I have to do?"

<*Right now, we're playing Kill the Babysitter. It's very easy to play. But I don't see any dead babysitters yet. The suspense is killing me!*>

"Why are you doing this?" Her teeth grit together.

<*Because it's a game, and I love games. But I love death even more.*>

"I don't want to hurt anybody."

<*But that's how you win. Don't you want to win?*>

"Not like that."

<*Boy, you sure brought the rain to my parade. The rules are kill or be killed.*>

Jane sobbed, choking on the smoke. *"No, please—"*

<*Either kill the babysitter or...*>

"Or what?"

The smoky figure's hands hovered over Barbie's shoulders. His face contorted into a grin.

<*Or she kills you.*> He leered at the side of her face. <*She looks like a cream puff, but I'll bet she's got one helluva killer instinct.*>

"Barbie?"

<*Your friend.*>

"She's not my friend."

<Good. Then this will be easier for you.>

Above, the door to the basement cracked open. Three sets of feet stormed downstairs. Jane heard them coming — *the Harker children* — but she wasn't afraid of them anymore. She was no longer going to let them have power over her, just as she wasn't going to let Zed and the Ouija board have power over her.

"It's just a game," she said.

<Then play it.>

Jane stared across at the bawling mess that was Barbie Stanley. The Beast. Just a regular girl caught in a communication breakdown. Maybe under better circumstances they would have been friends. When she really thought about it, Jane didn't have too many of those.

Because I'm an awful person.

I took this job from someone like Lily who would have been perfect. She wouldn't have let the kids play with the board and summon an evil spirit from beyond. She would have had them in bed at a reasonable hour. She wouldn't have been chasing dollar signs.

Same with Barbie. She's better than me too.

"It's over," she said. "It's a draw. No one else dies tonight."

<Kill the babysitter — it's your only way out.>

"No."

<Kill the babysitter, Jane.>

"I can't!" She realized she would never be better than Lily or Barbie, even if she lived through this and went on to become a nun and build hospitals for orphans until her

dying day — she would never be as kind hearted as the girl who trembled in front of her.

<Last chance. I can give you everything you've ever wanted. I can make you rich beyond your wildest dreams. I can even bring the boy back to life. I can—>

He rattled off everything Jane had ever wanted. Popularity, acceptance, a boyfriend, good grades, money without work, more time with her mom.

<Your every wish come true...>

None of it was enough for Jane to kill an innocent girl. She had already made her life a living hell — she didn't need to take it away from her too.

So she made a promise to herself. When this was all over, she was going to be kinder to people, especially Lily and Barbie, and she was going to be a better daughter to her mom. Maybe even clean out the storage shed as she was told.

"Goodbye," Jane said.

<You're no fun>

"Too bad."

<So let's see what the Beast decides!>

"What?"

The smoke dissipated in time for Jane to see Barbie burst forward. Her face was pale, her eyes red. And then Jane was choking — not on smoke, but a thick coppery liquid filling her throat. She grabbed her neck. Icy, electric pain jolted her. Her hands became wet with blood.

Gasping and sputtering, she leaned toward Barbie for help. *"Bar—"*

She slumped forward, bleeding on the Ouija board. Barbie pushed away from the coffee table, and as she did, she dropped her steak knife, dripping with Jane's blood.

Shaking, Barbie stood over her. "I'm sorry! I'm so sorry..."

But Jane wasn't mad. Just cold. She wanted to go home. She wanted her mom. She wanted this to be over. *I wish... I wish...*

But it was too late for wishes. Too late to take anything back. Too late to be a better person. Too late to win the game.

She exhaled, her heart beating one final time, and the last thing she saw was Barbie slide the planchette onto GOODBYE.

Barbie won. Barbie killed the babysitter.

AFTER

One month later...

Barbie passed through the cafeteria doors carrying her lunch bag, her backpack slung over one shoulder. One of the cutest boys in school smiled at her as she went by. "Hey, hero," he said.

She smiled back shyly. "Ha, thanks."

It was her first week back at school, and she was still getting her bearings in navigating this new world.

Everything was different after the fire.

After the Harker children called 911 and dragged her out of the basement, she was taken to the hospital and treated for smoke inhalation. The medical staff were impressed with her incredible recovery. It was almost too good to be true — at least that was what Nurse Tanis kept saying every time she came by to check on her. Tanis came around too often, with wide eyes and something on her mind. Eventually, her supervisor told Tanis to take a leave of absence. Then Barbie didn't have to see her anymore.

Barbie's mom and dad were so relieved she survived — unlike "that Freeman girl" — that they let her stay home for a few weeks to recover.

Her teachers weren't even mad. They sent Emily Burke to drop off her assignments and help her with homework, but Barbie caught up quickly, and that gave her and Emily time to talk and become friends.

The fire was the best thing that could have happened to her.

Barbie Stanley was a hero.

She saved the three Harker children from a devastating house fire that took the life of their babysitter, Jane. Barbie ran in and saved them in the nick of time. (And luckily she went over when she did because a drunk RCMP officer came speeding by, lost control of his squad car, and crashed into the Fowler house, where thankfully Jaxon and Jayden were safe in bed.)

But when she went back in for Jane, Barbie couldn't find her and got disoriented from all the smoke. Thankfully Olivia, Noah, and Emma came to her rescue. The four of them made it out of the house just as the emergency vehicles arrived.

Emily waved Barbie over to where she was eating with Brad Polanski, Mark Cote, and Nicole Albert. The cool kids table. Barbie smiled and headed their way. She wasn't surprised by the invite; in fact, she had been expecting it.

"Hey, hero," grinned Emily. "How ya feelin'?"

Barbie shrugged as she settled in between Brad and Mark. "Oh, you know…"

Mark shook his head as he shoveled his sandwich into his mouth. "Crazy, man. Just crazy."

"I mean, like, I didn't *know* Jane very well," said Nicole, tossing her silky hair off her shoulder, "but, like, she always seemed a little *off*, didn't she?"

Emily shushed her. "Don't speak ill of the dead."

"Come on, Em." Nicole rolled her eyes. "Jane always was kind of a monster."

The rest of the table nodded. Barbie kept her head down, rooting through her lunch bag for an apple. She didn't need to say anything. But as she looked up, she saw mousy Lily Clark, hugging her backpack as she peeked into the cafeteria for a place to sit. When they made eye contact, Lily frowned and ducked outside.

Barbie ignored her. Lily just missed Jane, that was all. There was nothing she could do about it, nothing she could change to bring her back — well, that wasn't entirely true. She just wasn't going to waste a wish on a bully. Lily would have to suck it up and find a new mean girl to hang out with.

But what if she knows? Barbie wondered. *No, no one will ever know. I covered my bases.*

* * *

Since her near-miss with Jane in that blue car months ago, Barbie had been frightened of running into her again. And when that driver hit her, she was certain Jane had something to do with it; she just couldn't prove it. She convinced herself to keep babysitting for the Fowlers and that she would be safe inside the house.

But all through the night, all she could think about was how much she hated Jane Freeman. She was the *real* beast. She ruined school for her and now her babysitting gig. She began to think she was going to have to quit and find somewhere else to go.

A voice deep inside asked, *Why should you be the one to leave? Why doesn't that miserable girl go away?*

Barbie tried to reason. Jane was obviously there first. Maybe she even lived in that house. No, that wasn't possible — that was the Harker family's house. So she must be babysitting.

Why would anyone trust her with children?

And then: *Maybe the world would be a much better place without her.*

She just about gasped out loud. No. That was a terrible thought. But the idea rooted itself, and up until the night she dragged Jane out of the street and away from the blood-thirsty Harker kids, she had let it germinate, imagining how much better life would be without a bully.

No one needs bullies. Like mosquitos, they serve no other purpose than to annoy (at best) or make life a living hell (at worst).

When Jane mentioned the Ouija board and the wishes,

Barbie didn't believe her. There was always a risk with trusting someone who calls you names behind your back and thinks you're a disgusting beast, but she also trusted her instincts that something supernaturally wrong had happened to the children. Barbie had to do something because she knew deep down that Jane wouldn't.

Bullies are cowards.

"Barbie? She's not my friend."

Barbie was surprised how much that stung. After everything they had been through in such a short time, Jane still managed to be cruel.

Well, I don't want to be your friend either.

In the books Barbie had read growing up, the characters — especially the ones that started out not liking each other — usually ended up best friends after going through situations like this. Barbie wasn't so lofty minded that she thought she and Jane would become BFFs, but she at least hoped the negativity and pain would stop. That they would settle somewhere in the area of mutual respect.

Turns out Jane was a bitch, even as they suffocated together in a burning building.

Had Barbie not also been offered the same chance to play the game as Jane, she would have simply cried and raged and felt frustrated that after everything they had been through, Jane hadn't changed the slightest bit.

<*See how she hurts you? Wouldn't you love to hurt her back? Wouldn't you love to win for once?*>

"Sh-she didn't mean it."

<Don't make excuses for your abuser. You're strong enough to do this. Just say the words... Play the game...>

"I-I don't know..."

<Don't let this wretched girl ruin your life.>

Barbie shook her head, whipping her hair around her face. "I'm not hurting anyone! Just go away. Goodbye!"

<You can have anything. Your foot fixed. Your popularity in bloom. The boyfriend of your dreams. Your enemies vanquished...>

"No, please..."

<All you have to do is play the game and make a wish.>

"I don't want to."

<I promise it will all be worth it. You'll never get a better deal than this one. Don't give up your only chance for a better life. One without this beast in it.>

Barbie stared hard at the board. The letters curled upward — or so it seemed — into a dark grin.

"I don't want to play."

<Then end the game by winning it — kill the babysitter. Don't let her beat you to it. Don't let her steal your chance at a perfect life.>

Barbie lifted the steak knife. Or rather, it felt like a shadowy hand guided her, wrapping her fingers around it.

<It'll be fun...>

Just as the smoke cleared and Jane's blank expression blinked back to reality, Barbie leapt up and slashed the knife across her throat. Her neck split open. Blood poured down her shirt and onto the Ouija board. It was the most horrifying scene Barbie had ever witnessed, but she forced herself to watch.

It was the least she could do.

"I'm sorry! I'm so sorry..."

<Make your wish, Barbie. Make your dreams come true... What do you want?>

* * *

All of it.

Emily gently nudged Barbie with her elbow. "You alright, Barb? You looked like you left your body."

"Is it PTSD?" asked Brad. "You know, after what happened?"

"No, I'm fine, really," said Barbie, looking up at the cute boy walking toward her. He smiled, carrying a blood-red rose. People in the cafeteria watched him, some even exclaiming, "OooOOooOOooh!"

Barbie had turned completely red by the time Nate Crawford squeezed in next to her. He put an arm around her shoulders and grinned, giving her the rose. She grinned back.

"Hi, beautiful," he said. "Missed you."

"We just saw each other this morning!" she said, giggling into her shoulder.

"Aww! You guys are so cute," gushed Emily.

"*So* cute," agreed Nicole.

Nate, as if sensing Barbie's discomfort at being the center of attention, leaned in and stole a carrot stick from

Emily's snack bag. Biting into it with a loud crunch, he asked, "What're we talking about?"

"Barbie saving those kids," said Brad.

"Bad ass," said Mark.

Barbie smiled sheepishly. She had saved Nate too — he just didn't know it. All he knew was that he woke up Saturday morning in his own bed with a terrible flu, phantom aches and pains, and a heart-wrenching crush on Barbara Stanley.

"Do you think, like, Jane *meant* to do something bad to those kids?" whispered Nicole.

"The Beast?" said Mark. "Sure, why not? We always knew she was fucked up."

"So weird, you guys. I totally forgot about this..." Nate brought up the texts on his phone and passed it around the table. "Jane texted me that night. I showed my folks and they showed the police."

Barbie's heart thundered. *No, no, no! I made a wish! I played the game. This isn't fair! Whatever this is—*

The phone came her way and she stopped to skim the messages as casually as she could. Relief washed over her, so powerful it would have brought her to her knees had she been standing.

Harker kids! They're the worst! I'm gonna MURDER THEM!

Clamping down on a shaky smile, she slid the phone back to Nate.

Emily was hung up on another detail. "You really offered to go hang out with her that night? Creepy."

"Yeah, I know," said Nate, looking at his phone. "Told you it was weird."

"Did you go?" asked Mark.

"Nah, I guess I just went to bed early. Was feeling pretty lousy all weekend. Lucky me, eh?" He grinned at Barbie again, pulling her closer.

She smiled back at him before Emily made a joke that made the table burst out laughing. Mark didn't get it and everyone dragged him for being dumb. Barbie relaxed.

I don't need luck, she said. *Not when I have an endless supply of wishes.*

Even though she told herself she had enough — all the children went back to normal, Nate was alive as her loving boyfriend, her foot had healed, and she gained a bunch of new best friends — she still couldn't help wondering what she was going to wish for tonight when she babysat the Harker kids in their new home.

Nate leaned in and kissed her. "What are you doing tonight?"

"I don't know," she said with a shrug. "Hoping to have some fun."

THE END

THANK YOU FOR READING!

Being an indie author is hard work, so I thank you for finding and reading my book. If you enjoyed it, please leave a review or tell a friend. Or review a friend and tell me about them. I like judging people.

— *S.S.*

ABOUT THE AUTHOR

Retro horror author Stephanie Sparks writes stories reminiscent of classic 70s and 80s slasher and monster movies. She loves scream queens, final girls, and the masked maniacs who stalk them. Her books feature action, thrills, dark humour, and sarcasm. She prefers cats to people, and when she's not lost in a paperback from hell or listening to 1980s movie soundtracks, she's daydreaming ideas for her next book or writing furiously.

See what she's working on at StephanieSparks.ca.

ALSO AVAILABLE

Scream, Queen
1984... Beautiful, do-good student Becca has been nominated for the coveted role of queen of her town's Harvest Festival. But when she starts looking into its history, she discovers that each of the past queens died under mysterious circumstances — including her mom. There is something insidiously rotten about the festival, and if Becca can't escape her queenly duties, she will have to make the ultimate sacrifice.

The Stepchildren
Jamie had always suspected something was wrong with her stepfather. Burt wasn't just a man on the hunt for the perfect life — he was a fugitive family annihilator. Years after surviving his attack, Jamie and his other stepchildren come together in group therapy where they learn he has died in prison. Or has he? Turns out, even in death, stepdaddy dearest has a few deadly surprises left for his wayward stepchildren.

See more at StephanieSparks.ca.

PREVIEW

THE STEPCHILDREN

"Call me Daddy," he said.

Fifteen-year-old Jamie Riley choked down the bland lump of cold, leftover wedding cake as she stared up at her stepfather, towering over her in his tan slacks and itchy sweater vest. It sure beat the obnoxiously white tuxedo he wore the day before. His muddy brown eyes bulged, magnified behind his thick-lensed glasses. Clutching a glass of warm milk, he rubbed at the milk mustache coating the bristles under his nose, not quite swiping it away.

The guy was a dork. From the day her mother sprang him on her — "Jamie, honey? I want you to meet someone" — to the moment he donned his wedding day best, Jamie rolled her eyes at his royal dorkiness.

At first, she paid him no mind, because he was just

another guy in her mother's long list of losers, following in her father's footsteps. She figured he wouldn't last.

Burt was not like the others. He proposed to Christine after three months of dating, though Jamie suspected they had kept their coupling a secret for a few months before telling her. They tittered like teenagers when Christine gave him a tour of the house — *their house. Not his.*

He strutted around the place, eyeballing their family photos and critiquing Jamie's drawings, like he was some high-brow art critic. He straightened the frames on the wall and wiped dust away with his index finger. He prowled about, taking everything in. Looming over the mother and daughter in the living room, he was too tall for their house. Simply, he wasn't a good fit.

"I'm not calling him anything," Jamie vowed the night before the wedding. She toyed with her mother's veil. The wedding itself was lavish and unnecessary, but Christine never got a dream wedding with Jamie's dad. They married in a friend's backyard a month before Jamie was born.

"You don't have to call him anything," Christine conceded. "Just Burt. And if one day you want to call him 'Dad,' that's okay too."

Jamie had a dad already. Just not a very involved one. Tanner Riley was a deadbeat husband who walked out on them when Jamie was only eight. He came back from time to time to pay up his child support and take Jamie for soft-serve ice cream down the street. But he never had any fatherly wisdom to impart or love to give. He was more like a fun uncle, grinding up all his money and energy into getting his band off the ground.

When Tanner walked out on them, Christine uprooted her daughter. She convinced her parents to help her buy a house in the Port Coquitlam neighborhood of Mary Hill with its rolling hills, established trees, and unique 70s-era homes.

They lived seven happy years there before Burt wiped his loafers on their welcome mat. The house became his almost overnight.

Jamie set aside the piece of cake, swiped from the fridge. A late-night snack for a late-night study session. Her mother may have just gotten married, but that didn't make her mountain of homework go away.

"Uh, what?" she asked as Burt reached across her desk and snatched the fork from her hand. "Hey!"

He forked himself a big bite, cramming the dessert into his mouth. Crumbs spewed out, littering her textbooks. Then he gulped down his milk, wiping his mouth with his thumb and forefinger, pinky and ring finger curled around the fork. His gold wedding band flashed. All the while, a whiny wind whistled through his nose.

"Mmm, that's good!" Then he added, "I just stopped in to say goodnight."

She rolled her eyes. "Goodnight, Burt."

"We're family now," he said. "Call me Daddy."

"Don't think so," she mumbled. Scowling, she reached for her sketchpad, hidden under her bio notes, and began scribbling. She hoped he would get the hint and go away.

"It's a little late for that, Jelly Bean," he said, pushing his nickname on her.

"Don't call me that."

Her desk lamp cruelly cast his long shadow against her door, making him even more imposing. "Time for lights out."

Ugh. Eye roll. "It's *only* eleven. And Mom lets me stay up as late as I want."

"Well, your mother and I had a discussion about that, and we think you would do better in school if you got the proper amount of sleep. A solid eight hours always does wonders for me."

"I'm trying to do my homework."

"It looks like you're doodling."

She shot him a frosty look. "It's for art class."

"Oh, really?" He raised an eyebrow over his dated frames, snatching the book out from under her. Her pencil scratched the paper, leaving a dark, unwanted, and impossible-to-erase mark. Her picture was ruined. Burt frowned, turning it from side to side. "I can't even tell what this is." He knocked on her bio textbook. "I'd recommend hitting these books. Art is not your ... strong point."

His opinion didn't hold water with her. Not only was he a dork, but he was a boring, old real estate agent who liked bugs. He didn't have an artistic bone in his body and he wouldn't know good art if it walked up and bit his nose.

Yet, the criticism stung.

"Give it back," she demanded.

He tucked the pad under his arm. "It's time for bed."

"Give it *back.*"

Shadows grew longer, deeper on his face. The reflection on his lenses masked his dark eyes. *"I won't tell you again."*

Grumbling, she jumped up from her desk and slammed the chair against it, which rattled the mirror against the wall and shook the lamp. She stormed to her bed, pulled back the comforter, and plopped down, arms crossed. "There. Happy now?"

He pointed to the lamp. "You forgot to turn out the light."

She puckered her face. "I want it on."

"I said it was time for lights out. Turn. Off. The. Light."

"Back off," she muttered. She knew how the words sounded coming out of her mumbling mouth, but she would never actually swear at an adult. Her mother would lose her shit. But Burt didn't know her well enough, just as she didn't know anything about him. Yet.

But he didn't yell or run off to tell her mother. He took two swift steps to her desk, wrapped his fist around her lamp, and marched off with it. The cord stretched, knocking her papers and books to the floor. As he left her room, he gave it one good, hard yank. Darkness blanketed the room.

Unsettled, she couldn't see where he had gone — until his breath hit her cheek. "Don't you ever *fuck* with me," he snarled. "And from now on, you call me Daddy. We're family now, so you better start acting like it."

He dropped the sketchpad on her thighs with a slap.

Then he left, the lamp cord trailing behind him.

She clutched the pad to her chest. *Fucking psycho,* she thought, tears threatening to spill.

She didn't know the half of it.

Want more?

Order your copy today:

Amazon
Barnes & Noble
Blackwell's
Booktopia
Kobo
Waterstones
And more…

CPSIA information can be obtained
at www.ICGtesting.com
Printed in the USA
LVHW030924060821
694358LV00002BA/112